The Golden Amazon

Book One of the Original Golden Amazon Saga

CU01426126

John Russell Fearn

To my esteemed friend
Professor A. M. Low

Table of Contents

History of The Golden Amazon by Philip Harbottle

JOHN RUSSELL FEARN was born in Worsley, near Manchester, England, on June 8th 1908. This was the very same year in which a giant meteorite crashed to earth in Siberia, causing a tremendous explosion and flattening several hundred miles of forest. It was therefore fitting that Fearn was to grow up to become a prolific writer of science fiction stories, specialising in tales of the Earth in danger of destruction—both from giant meteorites like the real-life one which fell in Russia, and from other more fanciful causes dreamed up by his fertile imagination.

As a young boy, Fearn became fascinated by science fiction, first by devouring the works of H. G. wells and Jules Verne, and then by reading the many tales of fantastic adventure appearing in the numerous Boy's Magazines and books which flourished in Britain between the wars, such as *Nelson Lee* and *The Boys' Friend Library*.

Fearn began his career as a published science fiction writer in America, when *Amazing Stories* serialized his first novel *The Intelligence Gigantic* in 1933. Over the next decade, Fearn sold more than 100 stories of all lengths, under his own name and numerous pseudonyms, to the leading SF magazines in both America and England. As versatile as he was prolific, he used a variety of styles that ranged from universe-destroying 'thought-variants' to intensely human stories.

In 1939 Fearn created science fiction's very first super-heroine (nearly two years, be it noted, *before* 'Wonder Woman'.) Fearn's heroine was called Violet Ray—alias 'The Golden Amazon'—and her exploits appeared in the American magazine *Fantastic Adventures*. After just four stories, Fearn completely revised his concept, jettisoning the Amazon's pulp origins. He upgraded his writing for the English hardcover market, producing what was in effect an entirely new character for his novel *The Golden Amazon*. This was printed as an original hardcover in 1944 by the World's Work press in England.

The following year, *The Golden Amazon* was reprinted as a 'Novel of the Week' in the Canadian magazine the Toronto *Star Weekly*. It proved so popular with its 900,000 readers that Fearn was commissioned to write an entire series of open-ended sequels, ending only with his death from a heart attack in 1960.

Although the Golden Amazon was Fearn's most famous and successful creation, the series of novels featuring her exploits has had a long and difficult history, and is only now achieving anything like the attention and respect it deserves.

During Fearn's lifetime, when he was able to promote the novels, the first six Amazon novels were re-issued in hardcover editions in England, published by the World's Work Ltd, between 1944 and 1954. Unfortunately World's Work then decided to switch from fiction to non-fiction, and so their hardcover science fiction series came to a premature end.

Fearn thought he had found another book publisher to continue the series in Harlequin Books, the leading Canadian paperback publisher. The first three titles appeared between 1953 and 1958, but thereafter Harlequin also decided on a sea change in their publishing programme—they switched entirely to romances! The three attractive Canadian paperback editions—particularly the first one, with an attractive cover by artist Bill Book (who had illustrated most of the *Star Weekly* editions)—are now amongst the most sought-after items by collectors, and are extremely valuable.

The Amazon series ended with Fearn's premature death in 1960, but for several years the *Star Weekly* commissioned leading American SF writers (working through the Scott Meredith Agency) to try and continue the Amazon series. All of their attempts were rejected; no one could duplicate Fearn's unique "popular" style. Until his death, Fearn was in fact the *only* writer of science fiction to be regularly published by the *Star Weekly*, and all his novels to 1955 (including detective and western, as well as science fiction) were reprinted in syndication by several American newspapers, in the Maine and New York areas. They were featured in the *Newark Sunday Star Ledger*, the *Long Island Sunday Press*, the *Bangor News*, and the *Bangor Sunday Commercial*. These editions are now even scarcer than the Canadian prints.

The Amazon series quickly passed into legend, sustained only in the memories of elderly Canadian and American magazine and newspaper readers.

It was not until the publication of my bio-bibliography of Fearn, *The Multi-Man* (1968), that the first complete listing of all Fearn's science fiction (including his 24 published "Amazon" novels) became known. There was an immediate flurry of interest in Fearn's work, and I was approached by Ron Graham, an Australian SF fan and business man, and asked to set up a new publishing company in England. Graham's idea was to publish a line of SF paperbacks, reprinting the best novels of Fearn, and to create a new science fiction magazine *Vision of Tomorrow*, The magazine was to be published as a paperback book. I accepted the position of Managing Editor of the new company, and approached the author's widow, Mrs. Carrie Fearn, from whom I was able to purchase an option on all 24 Amazon novels.

I succeeded in finding an interested established paperback publisher, Icon Books, who offered to co-publish all 24 Amazon novels, issuing them simultaneously, to create immediate impact. However, Ron Graham felt that this would be too expensive to risk, and declined their offer. Ron himself had already decided to make the trip to England, and unknown to me he had set up a meeting with Transworld Publishers shortly after his arrival in London. He was persuaded by them to delay our paperback line, in order to first establish *Vision of Tomorrow* as a fully-illustrated large-size monthly science fiction magazine,

Within weeks of successfully distributing the first issue in July 1969, Transworld suddenly and inexplicably reneged on their agreement, withdrawing completely. They handed the distribution over to New English Library Ltd, an established *book* publisher who had only just set up a magazine division. The new arrangement proved disastrous, and the magazine eventually failed after 12 issues because of totally inadequate distribution. A key factor was that the main UK magazine distributors, W.H. Smith refused to stock the magazine, because New English Library had no previous track record with them as magazine distributors.

In the interim, whilst *Vision* was still being published, my publisher had agreed with me to bring out a companion magazine, *Image of Tomorrow*, which would feature a complete "Golden Amazon" novel in each issue, and also carry both new and reprint short stories. The first issue was typeset, featuring Fearn's seventh Amazon novel, *Conquest of the Amazon*, with a cover and interior illustrations by *Vision* artist Eddie Jones.

It had been decided to start with this novel (# 7 in the chronological sequence) as the story was self-contained, and marked a new phase in the Amazon's career. Unlike the earlier stories it was not "dated"—it seemed a good place for new readers of the Amazon to start. The idea was to continue with the rest of the novels in sequence, and then commission another writer to continue the character. However, when—on my recommendation—the decision was taken to close *Vision* and withdraw entirely from New English Library, the magazine had to be aborted.

I agreed with Ron Graham that we would forget magazines, and revert to the original scheme and publish only paperback books. I threw myself into the task, travelling to all parts of the country, seeking advice from people already in the trade, and taking advantage of all the contacts and friendships I had built up during my *Vision* editorship. I secured an option on a series of paperback originals by John Wyndham, comprising two collections of short stories, *Wanderers of Time* and *Sleepers of Mars*, which had never appeared in book form in either England or America, and two 1930s novels, *Stowaway To Mars* and *The Secret People*, which were long out of print, and had previously only appeared under the pen name of 'John Beynon'. Wyndham had died at the height of his fame the previous year, and so publication under the "John Wyndham" byline for the first time meant that these four titles would be received by the trade *as brand new John Wyndham books*, thus assuring them of massive sales. I showed my proposed programme to one of Britain's most successful publishers, Gordon Landsborough (creator of the phenomenally successful Panther Books and Four Square Books amongst other companies), whom I had earlier met at the 1970 British Science Fiction Convention in London.

Landsborough was so impressed with my proposed opening publishing programme of "Graham SF Classics"—Wyndham, E.C. Tubb, William F. Temple, Jack Williamson, A.E. Van Vogt, to eventually be followed by Fearn's "Golden Amazon" series—that he offered his services as an unpaid adviser to the line. Using his own contacts in the publishing world, he secured for me a deal with the largest paperback printer in the U.K. (on the same advantageous discounted terms he was receiving for his own company, Dragon Books). He also introduced me to his friend Ralph Stokes, who had successfully launched the publishing firm of

Tandem Books. Tandem agreed to act as UK distributor for the new line of paperbacks.

The deal was essentially similar to one that Don Wollheim would create many years later with the New American Library (for "DAW Books" substitute "Graham Books"). Contracts and options were prepared and everything was set to go. The plan was to open with the four "block-buster" John Wyndham titles, which were assured of national distribution by W. H. Smith and other big book chains (thus overcoming the problems which had killed *Vision of Tomorrow*).

All it needed was the money to print the four Wyndham titles, after which Tandem's advance would be sufficient to pay the agreed advance on royalties to the Wyndham estate. Thereafter, the line should be self-financing.

Ron replied angrily to the effect that "It's my money, and I'm entitled to publish anything I like. If I can't publish whatever titles I want, and have to publish only stuff acceptable to W. H. Smith, why should I publish anything?"

It was a perfectly good question, to which I could only think of one answer. I sent him my resignation. The line was aborted, and my hoped-for career in science fiction book publishing was over before it had started. I resumed the Local Government career I had been obliged to leave to form the new company.

I saw Mrs. Fearn at her Blackpool home personally in order to explain how things had gone wrong. She graciously thanked me for my efforts in trying to restore the Amazon series to print, and asked me to become her literary agent. She also gave me the mss of two unpublished Amazon novels, and a brief outline of an unwritten 27th book (which I would later write myself as a posthumous collaboration.)

Ron Graham's time-limited option on the Amazon novels (which he never exercised) eventually ran out, and all rights in them reverted to Mrs. Fearn. The first thing I did was to issue *Conquest of the Amazon* in a limited edition myself, as an A4 chapbook. I used this for promotional purposes to send to prospective publishers.

When I had taken over Fearn's representation for his widow, the publishing climate (pre-POD, and pre-Ebook) was totally different to what it is today. There were hardly any small independent publishers, and the whole science fiction publishing climate was hostile to publishing older science fiction that was "out of date" or scientifically disproven, i.e. breathable air on Venus, and Martians, etc. There were, of course, a handful of exceptions, such as Verne, Wells and E.R. Burroughs, who had been accorded special "classic" status. But the rank and file older SF author was barred from mainstream republication where their stories had become astronomically outdated.

However, the Golden Amazon series fell into two different phases, Books 1 to 6 (all written in the 1940s) were astronomically outdated and "impossible". But books 7 onwards were set further into the future, in *interstellar* space and other solar systems and so were possible or at least could not be disproved. Those *were* publishable. And, equally importantly, numbers 7 onwards *had never been published in book form*—only as Canadian and American newspaper supplements. Thus I was soon able to place book # 7 with Futura, then one of the leading SF publishers in the UK. *Conquest of the Amazon* went on to be twice reprinted in UK paperback, first by Futura in 1975, and later by Trojan Books in 1986. However Futura did not continue with the rest of the Amazon series as originally agreed. They had appointed a new editor, who decided to publish the German space opera series *Perry Rhodan* instead.

There were also two authorised comic strip versions of the Amazon. The first, adapted and drawn by artist David Lloyd, was a short 'pilot' version of the opening chapters of *The Golden Amazon*, which appeared in *Warrior* in 1982. It was excellently done, but Lloyd achieved a greater success with a second strip in the same magazine, "V for Vendetta" and perforce had to drop the Amazon in order to concentrate on this other strip thereafter. It was an international success and was later filmed.

The second version was by artist Ron Turner, who drew a full-length graphic novel adaptation of *Conquest of the Amazon* in 1984, from a script written by myself. But the prospective publisher failed, and the graphic novel was fated to only appear from a small press in a chap-book edition.

In 1991, at my instigation the eighth 'Amazon' novel, *Lord of Atlantis*, was issued as a limited edition chapbook by Zeon Books, a UK Small Press. It was my hope that these small press editions would eventually attract a larger publisher to reissue the entire Golden Amazon series.

In due time, the SF publishing climate became more enlightened, its readership base wider and less critical, and willing to suspend disbelief *in order to be entertained by sheer good story telling, rather than scientific accuracy.* Small publishers sprang up, catering for niche and collector markets. I went to New York touting my clients E.C. Tubb and Fearn (and all their unpublished in book form work) and sold their works to Gary Lovisi's Gryphon Books, a New York Small Press who aimed at the Collector's market —including the entire 27 book Amazon series.

I deliberately ceded only non-exclusive single edition paperback rights, limited to 500 copies. After the books had been published, I knew they would eventually attract interest from larger publishers, and I wanted to be able to offer them elsewhere. Such was the case when I was approached by the late Michael Burgess, heading Borgo Books, an imprint of Wildside.

Notwithstanding the more liberal publishing climate, I still considered that in order to re-boot the Amazon series to a wider market, the Amazon stood a better chance if I started it with book 7 (retitled as "World Beneath Ice") and the "non-impossible, far-future interstellar" phase. There were two distinct phases in the Amazon books. Books 1 to 6 were set in the (then) near future and the action limited to the solar system. With book 7 Fearn had introduced a new character, Abna of Alantis. The Amazon married him, and left Earth with him and their daughter Viona, calling themselves 'the Cosmic Crusaders'. Not only was the locale changed from the solar system to the stars, but the entire tenor of the books too. An introductory article in the Borgo editions explained that their series was being renumbered to start with No 1 (but was actually No.7; 2 was 8, 3 was 9, and so on,)

At the time, Gryphon still had some copies of their 500 copy editions of the Amazon unsold (chiefly the earlier books that had previously appeared from other publishers). I was grateful to Lovisi (by then a personal friend) and so took the decision to withhold books 1 to 6 from Borgo, to help Lovisi to sell out his print run.

Then fate intervened. Hurricane Katrina struck New York, and flooded Lovisi's Brooklyn home *destroying his entire stock* of Gryphon Books. This destruction included all his unsold Amazon books! *This has served to make the first six Golden Amazon novels extremely rare collectors' items, putting them out of print.*

So when I was introduced to Endeavour Press and Venture Books, with their enlightened editorial policy of publishing both contemporary *and* classic science fiction it was the perfect home to restore the original Golden Amazon to print!

Readers can now look out for the *original* Golden Amazon, available only in the following Venture book editions:

Adventure # 1 The Golden Amazon
Adventure # 2 The Golden Amazon Returns
Adventure # 3 The Golden Amazon's Triumph
Adventure # 4 The Amazon's Diamond Quest
Adventure # 5 The Amazon Fights Again
Adventure # 6 Twin of the Amazon

Each of the books will contain my introductory essays offering insights and sidelights on each of these six Amazon novels, in chronological order. As a life-long collector, and researcher into Fearn's life and work, I hope they may add to the reader's enjoyment and appreciation of the stories.

Introducing "The Golden Amazon"

John Russell Fearn's famous sf heroine the 'Golden Amazon', originally made her fictional debut in a novelette in the July 1939 issue of *Fantastic Adventures* magazine. Readers voted the story "best in the issue", prompting editor Ray Palmer to ask for sequels. Three more novelettes appeared during the early years of the war, under Fearn's "Thornton Ayre" pseudonym. Written to the "fast action" pulp formula demanded by Palmer, the prototype Amazon had a "Tarzanesque" origin.

Sole survivor of a spaceship crash on Venus, the baby Violet Ray is brought up by native "Hotlanders." The Venusian climate turns her into a golden-skinned superwoman.

At maturity, the girl becomes a lone-wolf avenger, dedicated to smashing the criminal gang who had killed her parents by causing their spaceship to crash. The Amazon was a distinctly unusual heroine, meting out her own ruthless justice to her enemies—usually by strangling them with her bare hands. But this Amazon still had her normal human side, and in the pulp version she marries an ordinary Earthman, astronomer Chris Wilson, and has twin children (super-strong, like herself.)

Fearn's original intention seems to have been to continue the series by featuring the adventures of her grown up children, with the widowed Amazon restricted to cameo appearances. But in 1943, Fearn courageously decided to quit writing for the American pulps, and launched upon a successful bid to achieve British hardcover book publication, upgrading his writing in the process.

Writing in 1948, Feam recalled: "Throughout the war years the idea remained that she (the Amazon) was too good to lose, so I decided to make a full-length book about her."

Jettisoning her entire pulp background, Fearn made sweeping changes for his novel. "In the first novel about her published by World's Work in April 1944, she was a baby lost in the Blitz, operated upon by a super-surgeon. He changed her glandular structure, which—at maturity—would mean she would have more than human strength, abnormally brilliant intelligence, and an almost sexless outlook on life. The surgeon's idea was that she would lead the world to eternal peace, but he had miscalculated and her incredible knowledge of science led her to practically destroy the world by her finding of atomic power."

Significantly, the book was dedicated "to my Esteemed Friend Professor A.M. Low." Archibald Montgomery Low (1888-1956) was a Scot, and a graduate of the Imperial College of Science and Technology, London University. Low became an expert in acoustic research, successfully photographing sound waves in 1912. In 1914, he invented and patented a system of television, and during the war invented and built the first radio-robot plane, developed as a flying bomb. His life was devoted to scientific research, and he served with distinction during World War Two, working for the Air Ministry. He is credited with producing new explosives, radio inventions, and rocket-carrying aeroplanes. Author of three sf novels, he was one-time Chairman of the British Interplanetary Society, and towards the end of his life contributed many articles to *Authentic Science Fiction*.

Fearn had first met Low in London, in April 1938, when they were both guests at the Second Annual British Science Fiction Convention. Both were nominated as President of the British Science Fiction Association; Low won the vote. They became friends, and throughout the war Fearn had kept in touch by correspondence. The dedication of his novel indicates that Fearn had thoroughly researched the book's highly-scientific background.

One of the most remarkable elements in the novel was Fearn's anticipation of Laser surgery, employed by Professor Axton on the baby girl who becomes the Amazon. Axton explains his methods:

"To put it briefly, I don't use knives at all: I use rays. Like this..." He picked up a tube-like instrument and depressed its handle gently between finger and thumb. Prout watched fascinatedly as from it there jetted a hair-thin ray of blinding brilliance, steel-blue in shade. He felt a strong inclination to protest as Axton directed it downward with a rock-steady hand towards the motionless child. There was something uncanny about the way the ray cleaved through the flesh and left a perfectly clean, bloodless line everywhere it traced.

"You see?" Axton glanced up momentarily and switched off. "This is pure bloodless surgery, the dream of our profession... No need for excessive blood loss— Instant sealing of the veins, arteries and capillaries until the job is done."

The novel's speculations about ductless glands were very much in line with contemporary scientific thinking and research at that time. Fearn also dealt engrossingly with issues of militant feminism, decades before these issues became part of modern society and debate.

The sheer quality of the novel attracted the attention of the prestigious Toronto *Star Weekly*. The Canadian magazine issued a complete weekly novel in newsprint format, running to 40-45,000 words. They were frequently original novels, proclaimed as "Never before published." When they reprinted Fearn's *The Golden Amazon* in 1945, it proved a sensation with their predominantly female readership. Fiction Editor Gwen Cowley commissioned Fearn to write sequels, and over the next 16 years, another 23 novels were first published in the *Star Weekly*.

CHAPTER I

It was the third time the two famous specialists had completed a circuit of the grounds, but so intent were they on their conversation they had but little awareness of the flowers and trees about them drooping in the hot September sunshine. The pair of them kept their eyes fixed on the gravel at their feet, each pondering the remarks of the other.

In appearance they were strikingly dissimilar. Dr. James Axton was tall, hawk-faced, nearly bald-headed, with loose fitting tweeds bagging about his bony six foot three. Ever and again he raised a thin, skilful hand to emphasise some point: it was a hand indeed which had probed the entrails of more than one famous personage.

His companion, Dr. Alfred Prout, was a foot less in stature, fresh-complexioned, blue eyed, with a shock of fair hair and a breast pocket which bristled with fountain pens and clinical instruments.

In the main, Dr. Axton was doing the talking, and its subject had been important enough, engrossing enough, to demand a triple circuit of the extensive grounds. But now Axton came to a halt, hands in trouser pockets, and looked earnestly down at his companion.

"Well, Prout, there it is. What do you think of it?"

Prout shook his head doubtfully. "I can't believe it! I just can't! You ask me here especially to give me details of your discovery and then as good as outrage my medical knowledge with your statements. Strength of ten men indeed! Really, Axton!"

"I expected your disbelief," Axton said, with a little sigh. "And you are justified in it until I have proved my point ..." His voice ceased for a moment as his eyes looked upwards at the blue of the summer sky. Far away to the south, thirty miles perhaps, the cloudless expanse was defiled by crisscrossing feathers of condensation. Dozens upon dozens of them ...

"Fools," Axton muttered, half to himself. "Blind, senseless fools!"

"At least," Prout said, "they are defending us. War is the game of fools; I admit it. Like any sane man I hate it. Only there it is ..."

He stopped talking, lost in sudden meditation. And in the hush of the grounds there came the far distant droning of aircraft, the rhythmic clicking of machine-gun fire, and at intervals the reverberation of falling bombs.

"There are never any victors," Axton said soberly. "The Battle of London, Prout. We should be proud to gaze upon it! To some, I suppose, it is the thrill of a lifetime. But to me, to you, to thousands of others, it is only crass idiocy ..."

Prout still remained silent. Axton, he knew, had sound reasons for his bitterness. Dunkirk had claimed his only son in whom every idea had been fostered. From that moment onward Axton had changed incredibly, had worked with ceaseless energy upon some mysterious research of his own, until now he had this startling idea for stopping all future wars ...

Prout suddenly restored attention to the subject as Axton's eyes remained fixed on that distant area of white streaked death.

"You say you have a way to give any living thing a strength of ten times normal, Axton. As a doctor I'd say you are crazy: as your friend I am prepared to listen to you, chiefly because I cannot imagine the great Axton making such a statement without a very sound reason."

Axton lowered his eyes and gave a colourless smile.

"I mean what I say — every bit of it. It was the loss of my own boy which started me on my search. I felt that there must be a way to stop this utter insanity. It was a conviction which deepened to a positive obsession after I had seen the sufferings of the civilians in these hellish air-raids on London. I racked my brains for an idea. Somewhere there had *got* to be a way to stop this madness ... I confess I thought of many fantastic things, all of them too airy, too high flown, to be of the least practical use. Finally I arrived at the conclusion that there is no method of stopping *this* war short of the way we are adopting — a fight to a finish. On the merits and demerits of this I am not concerned — but I *am* concerned with stopping it in the future. And, medically, it can be done!"

Prout raised an eyebrow. "But, man alive, how can the gift of ten times normal strength avert future wars? It seems to me that men so powerful would be more inclined to fight than ever!"

"Men *would*!" Axton agreed, smiling grimly. "Give almost any boy as much as a single wheel and he will probably spend his time rolling it over garden insects. If he is too old for that he will determine how best to make it into a juggernaut to kill his fellows and gain power. The future peace of the world does not rely on men, Prout. It is in the hands of women."

"Limitation of births, refusal to give children to the cause of war …?" Prout shrugged. "That view carries no real weight, Axton. Life goes on, wars or no wars. Fear of possible future wars will never stop the inevitable evolution of man, woman, offspring."

"You are a good doctor, my friend — but hear me out. Let us suppose that the future gave to the world a woman with the strength of ten men, the science of Einstein, and the will of an Oliver Cromwell?"

"A dream, Axton — and for a specialist, an incredible one!"

"No — a fact! That is the secret I found — the idea for which I searched with such desperation." Axton drove his right fist into his left palm emphatically. "As a specialist, with a vast knowledge of anatomy, I became suddenly aware how easily a young human being can be moulded into almost any pattern one might desire. Not by environment, not by social culture, not by anything of that nature. But by control of the glands — the ductless glands."

Prout was silent. He was on unsure ground here, for Axton was one of the greatest glandular specialists in the profession. If any man understood glands inside out, he did.

"The science of ductless glands is nothing novel," Axton went on, after a pause. "The veriest layman knows in these days that the glands are the main controllers of our temperaments and physique. Think of the number of men who suffer from a hardening of the arteries because of the excess of adrenalin produced by the suprarenal glands. Think how certain racial characteristics are brought about through glandular secretion. At random, take the Chinaman. The oblique eyes, the yellow skin, the stolid indifference to pain and in inflicting it … The pituitary glands near the root of the nose are almost entirely responsible. And so on, Prout. You know, as a doctor, that an adjustment of the pituitary glands can give to a human being a strength of ten times normal."

"Which reminds me of the record of the Norse fighter of long ago," Prout said, rather grimly. "Remember the Berserk who had the strength of ten men and was horrifyingly ugly? The skeleton of such a being dug up has shown that he suffered from a progressive disease of the pituitary which gave gigantic strength but which caused a corresponding ugliness.

Any physician knows that pituitary disease gives giant strength, but that it also brings an enlargement of the cheekbones and causes a vast hairiness of the face."

"The technical name for which disease is acromegaly," Axton nodded, with something of the indulgence one might show to a young student of medicine.

"Just the same, I begin to see your idea," Prout said, thinking. "Various glands are responsible for strength, energy, endurance, mental genius, and so on ... Some Russian scientists have indeed already made glandular experiments, Hivinoff for one — but the results have been hideous. Hideous, Axton! I have seen authentic photographs at the Institute of these literally vivisected beings. They are no longer even human in appearance. Create strength, and you destroy the mental balance: create the power of terrific, burning energy and the body dries rapidly into a charred and leathery shell. Produce infinite stoicism to pain and you have a Mongolian type of fiendish cruelty and revolting ugliness which soon dies. No, only Nature can maintain an even balance of the glands. Alter them in any degree and you have a sub-normal freak." Prout broke off with an irritated gesture. "You laugh, Axton! Why? Have I not stated medical truth?"

"Certainly you have. In fact you have positively excelled yourself. But what you have not done is draw a distinction between Russian scientists and James Axton."

"My dear chap, it is not necessary for me to point out such a distinction. I do not doubt that your ability to handle glands is far above that of any Russian experimenter, but I do say that either in your hands or theirs the results are bound to be identical in their hideousness. One cannot defeat Nature."

"Without any proofs I rather expected you'd say all this," Axton remarked, his gaunt face devoutly serious. "In fact I would not think much of you as a doctor if you hadn't ... But come with me a moment. I think I have something which will interest you ..."

He turned and led the way back to the house, then down into the basement laboratory he maintained privately. Switching on the light he went down the aisle between the benches and banks of instruments and scientific paraphernalia. Finally he paused at a large cage.

Prout studied it in some astonishment. It was an unusual cage, framework made entirely of cast iron with braced corner brackets for additional strength. The bars were bluey, glittering, and at least an inch thick … Then something stirred in the straw and Prout found himself looking at a small monkey.

"Would you say he is in any way different from an ordinary monkey? In appearance or alertness?"

Axton turned his gaunt face to his colleague as he asked the question.

"Well … no." Prout made the admission slowly for he had a pretty good idea of what was coming.

"In every way he has retained all his normal characteristics," Axton went on. "I have given him the strength of a gorilla, yet he has in no wise turned into a hideous travesty. Nor will he indeed … You observe the strength of the cage? And the bars are chrome steel, the strongest obtainable. Now, look here —"

Axton turned and picked up a bar of iron about two inches thick and a foot long. He tossed it into the cage and then watched in brooding silence as those tiny monkey hands seized it, twisted it mischievously, curled it into all manner of shapes with the simplicity of a man bending a warm candle.

It was impossible, of course. It was a trick. It had to be a trick, Prout told himself. He dare not believe this. It tore up all medical ethics by the roots.

"Could — could I see that bar?" he asked abruptly.

Axton gave a dry smile and retrieved it from the cage with a pair of tongs. Prout grabbed it, pulled and tugged with all his force without in the least straightening it out. Rather shamefaced, he tossed it down.

"I'm sorry, Axton. But somehow I expected …"

"A trick?" Axton asked gravely. Then he shook his head. "You had better get rid of your conservative ideas, Prout, and admit that you are gazing on something new in medical science. For you are, believe me!" He paused a moment, chin sunk on chest, regarding the monkey. Then he gave a shrug. "You have the proof now. The rest is up to you. I want you to sponsor me at the Medical Research Institute. I cannot do it for myself, of course. All I want is the permission of the research experts to experiment on a human being."

"Naturally I'll do my best, but — Look here, how the devil do you *do* it?" Prout demanded. "How do you manage to get gland adjustments so exact as to produce just the right effect without a harmful reaction?"

"I may show you sometime. For the moment let us call it my especial secret."

"But *what* a secret! And yet — and yet I cannot quite see your object in all this. You mentioned a little while ago something about a superwoman to end future wars. Isn't that taking rather a limited view with such a vast potentiality in your hands?"

"Limited?"

"Well, think of what you could do in other directions! Suppose it could be arranged that a selected number of male children were given over to the State at specified periods — children considered fit in every physical detail, that is — which in turn could be handed over to you and an army of gland-manipulators whom you have trained. Think of it! In time — twenty years anyway — there would be a race of supermen, gigantically strong, enduring, scientific —"

"In other words the nucleus of a new warring faction," Axton interrupted grimly. "To give a chosen number of men the elixir of the gods is just asking for it! This war now raging would seem footling by comparison."

"But they can maintain the *peace* of the world! They will have the power in their hands to do it."

Axton shook his head. "In the best of men, save one — who gave the world the only law it really need know today — there lies the lust for power. Gratify that lust, give a man supreme power over his fellows, and he will not be able to resist the urge to dominate. At least it is so in ninety per cent of men … Given a group of men, as you have suggested, and the effect is simply multiplied … So, my friend, as I said a little while ago, no man must ever know this secret. To the best of my belief, the safety of the future world can only be found in the hands of a woman — not several of them; just one. For I believe she will of her own accord gather to herself those of her own sex whom she feels she can trust. In woman, Prout, there is a beauty of soul, a depth of understanding altogether lovely which the finest of men can never attain. I know my own sex — its barbarity, its lusts, its demoniacal cruelty. Men have ruled the world for long enough — and look where it has got us!"

"I am not one of those men who deride a woman because she *is* a woman," Prout said. "But I do feel that you are unduly harsh on men. There are many who deserve nothing but praise. Also I think you will condemn this hypothetical woman of yours — providing you ever make the experiment — to a devastating amount of criticism and abuse."

"I know, and that is why I intend to give her such gifts — a physical and mental armour as it were — to withstand any and every onslaught which may be made upon her ..." Axton paused a moment, reflecting. Then he gave a wry smile. "Funny you should moot the idea of a group of male children to be taken by the State for the sole purpose of turning them into supermen. That very suggestion was made to me only recently by a European country. Somehow agents have got to know of my experiments and I was offered two million pounds, English value, for a complete dossier of my method."

"And how was your refusal taken?"

"Not very well, I'm afraid." Axton raised his eyes to the basement's tiny windows, gazed through them on to the distant streaks of vapour in the sky. "I have little doubt, Prout, that I am a marked man. The enemy agents who contacted me must know all about me, the position of this laboratory — everything. I have no illusions. One night, or one day, a carefully aimed bomb will try to destroy my life's greatest work ..."

Abruptly Axton turned, his lean face suddenly masked with the strain of his emotion.

"That is why matters are so urgent, Prout! I've got to make this experiment on a baby girl before it becomes too late. Without the sanction of the Medical Research Institute, I stand the risk of debarrment if I dare to operate. Of course, driven to desperation, I might do many things, but first I prefer the normal course of action. That is why I need all the help you can give me."

"You shall have it!" Prout declared earnestly. "The moment I leave here I will call on Dr. Henry Meller and make the necessary arrangements. For the life of me I cannot see how they can refuse your request."

"No?" Axton gave a tired, whimsical smile. "I wonder ..."

CHAPTER II

Dr. Prout, stimulated by the amazing thing he had witnessed on the part of the transformed monkey, succeeded in his efforts to secure a meeting of the Medical Research Institute in spite of wartime demands on the members' time. It was convened to take place in three days, and once he knew of the decision Axton went to work compiling a dossier of his entire experiment.

Whenever he had the time, Prout came along to assist him, and in his feverish energy and irritable contempt for trifles he glimpsed something of the anxiety possessing him. In fact it was something more than anxiety; it was a real fear that in spite of all the evidence he had to offer medical science, its tradition might still frown upon him as an outsider.

On the appointed day, however, he was complete master of himself. Meeting him in the ante-room of the Institutes Debating Chamber before they went in together — a necessity since Prout was the sponsor — Prout found him grave and calm, immaculately dressed, his leather-bound dossier under his arm. They limited themselves to a mere exchange of greetings; the issues ahead were too immense to permit of much indulgence in pleasantries.

Side by side they entered the Debating Chamber and took their seats in the front row. Axton laid his dossier on his knees, held it in his grip, while his gaze went round the semicircles of faces turned towards him. He and Prout sat as it were in the opening of a horseshoe, while in three tiers looking down upon them were the experts of the medical profession who were to pass judgment.

Some of them Axton recognized and felt he could count on their support. The others were not so familiar and were either studying him with professional interest or were gazing in thoughtful silence in front of them … Only in the bottom row was there a break in the line of seated men. Here stood a table, and behind it, waiting for the hush of commencement, was Dr. Henry Meller himself, President of the Institute.

Presently he came to life, smoothed a delicate, womanlike hand over his black hair, then aimed bushy dark eyebrows to either side of him. The impassive granite of his face took on an earnestness as he hammered loudly for silence.

"Gentlemen, the meeting is called to order!"

He waited a moment until the murmuring died into pin-quiet silence, then turned his steel grey eyes to Prout.

"Dr. Prout, as sponsor you will kindly state your reason for convening this meeting and introduce the member who desires to place his case before us. Proceed, please."

Prout got to his feet, pushed back his chair with a noisy squeak on the polished floor. He spoke quietly but clearly with the assurance of a man long accustomed to facing the absolute scrutiny of doctors.

"To the best of my belief, gentlemen, it has fallen to me to have the privilege of sponsoring the greatest worker in medical research since Pasteur or Lister. In introducing to you Doctor James Axton I am not asking for a hearing for just another investigator into medical mysteries, but for the closest attention to a discoverer whose name must go down among the immortals of pathological research. I know I can rely on fairness, gentlemen … Doctor James Axton —"

Prout motioned with his hand and then sat down again. Axton rose with the studied calm of a man who has been lost in deepest speculations. He laid his dossier on his chair, then with hands holding his coat lapels he gazed round once more on the attentive assembly as though making a final assessment of interest … There was not a sound in the great room.

"Gentlemen, the nature of the experiment I have made is worldwide in its implication, so unusual in its implication indeed that I realise I am almost bound to incur a great deal of incredulity from you … It involves a complete research into the ductless glands, my work beginning where that of Hardy and Lancaster left off some years ago. We all remember the rage there was at one time about so-called 'monkey glands,' the wishful thought being that the medical profession has perhaps at last found the elixir of eternal youth. We remember that in its proper perspective this discovery was reduced to simple gland control … And, turning to less fantastic fields, we all know that hardening of the arteries can be prevented by cutting off the supply of adrenalin to the victim …"

There was a general nodding of heads. Axton waited a moment, then drove straight to his point.

"Gentlemen, I have evolved a complete gland control of any human being, a form of surgery handled by instruments of my own designing. We know that the thyroid gland makes for intelligence: I can adjust it to produce genius ahead of anything we know today! The supra-renal glands produce strength and energy: I can also handle those so that the strength and energy can be increased ten-fold! The parathyroid gland is mainly responsible for age: that too I can rule so that life can be prolonged nearly seventy years beyond the normal span. The energy and beauty of youth will remain until well on in middle life. Ugliness, freakishness, all the supposed ill-effects attendant on such an experiment are dispensed with by my method."

"You are sure of this?" Meller asked slowly. "You can prove it?"

"To the hilt. I have a monkey in my laboratory at this very moment as the living example of my work. It has undergone treatment —"

"I can corroborate that," Prout interjected.

Sir Henry spread his hands. "Then why did you not bring this monkey here?"

"Because I dare not trust it outside its cage! With the strength of a gorilla and an almost human intelligence I dared not take the chance of bringing it here. But if you will come — or at least a committee of you — to my laboratory–"

"Really, Dr. Axton, you expect unlimited concessions, do you not?" Sir Henry asked irritably. "To convene this meeting at all under the present emergency conditions was difficult enough: the further demands you make simply cannot be acceded to."

"But," Axton said, astonished, "it is the only way in which I can prove my point! How else am I to do it?"

"Doctor Axton," Meller leaned over the table earnestly. "Doctor Axton, you tell us of your accomplishments in the field of ductless glands. We don't doubt your word because we know your reputation — but if, as you say, you have given to a monkey the strength of a gorilla and a subhuman intellect, of what avail is it? Surely you did not have this meeting convened purely to tell us that?"

"No ... Not just for that." Axton's voice was grim now. He had little difficulty in sensing the President's mood. "I convened this meeting to ask permission from you all to experiment on a human being — a female child of not more than three years of age."

If Axton had hoped to create a sensation he could not have done better. There was an instant hum of conversation and face turned quickly to face. Then again Meller restored order.

"Do we understand that you hope to create a human being in every way superior to a normal one?" he demanded in amazement.

"You do, Dr. Meller. A woman, who in twenty years will reach a finer maturity than any ever known before. A woman of rare beauty, vast intelligence, and the strength and endurance of a tigress!"

"But why do you seek to create such a woman?"

"To preserve the peace of the world for posterity!"

At that Meller sat back and smiled to himself. Then his bushy eyebrows jerked to the men on either side of him. They nodded a slow acquiescence to his obvious thoughts.

"I see," he said at last, slowly. "To preserve the peace of the world! A gland experiment tested out on a monkey — presumably because its physical structure is the nearest to that of a human being — is to be tried out on a hapless baby girl just to satisfy a whim! There have been many pacifists in the world of medicine, Doctor Axton, but few so original as you!"

Prout jumped to his feet, flushed with rage.

"This is outrageous! Before you even have the experiment fully outlined to you, you are ready to condemn!"

Dr. Meller's cold eyes narrowed at him, gazed at him, until he sat down again. Only then did Meller glance back to Axton.

"Perhaps, Doctor Axton, you would care to satisfy our natural curiosity by explaining exactly how you work?"

"In no circumstances!" Axton retorted. "My process remains a secret, but in this dossier" — he lifted it up in his hand — "is contained every detail of the effect produced, medical facts which not one of you can gainsay. My sole aim is to give to the world of the future a woman capable of enforcing perpetual peace."

"A strange belief indeed," Meller remarked drily. "As I see it — as most of us see it in fact — peace is the last thing we could expect with a superwoman in control. The inefficiency of womankind is notorious! One has but to drive along a highway behind a woman driver to be assured of that …"

He broke off and looked round on the smiling faces. Axton clenched his fists.

"Isn't that rather — irrelevant?" he asked acidly.

"At least, my dear Doctor, it is a fact of which we are all aware. No, you have the wrong idea. Woman — super or otherwise — can never be a benefit to the community. Do you imagine they would be paid less than men and given positions inferior to men if their skill was really so high?"

"I had overlooked, sir, that in addition to being a bachelor you are also a misogynist," Axton replied bitterly. "And in any case it is neither my purpose nor yours to discuss the abilities of womankind. All I wish to bring to your notice is the ghastly mess men have made of things today. For that reason more than any other I withhold my experiment from man, as a sex, and intend to confer it on a girl-child if I can but secure the permission."

There was a long silence while the assembly debated in whispers. Axton sat down and waited, studying the sardonic smile on Sir Henry Meller's thin lips ... Then presently he spoke again.

"I think I speak for everybody here, Doctor Axton, when I say that you ask the impossible. In the first place, you refuse to reveal your method of procedure, will not even describe the instruments you intend using. For that reason alone — though there are other factors of course — we cannot possibly take the responsibility of entrusting a living child to you. Between a little girl and a monkey there is, you must admit, an infinity of difference in physical structure. An experiment quite harmless to the iron constitution of a monkey might easily kill a female child ... In the second place, your desire to create a super-woman to control the future destiny of mankind is at the best nothing but a personal and somewhat eccentric ideal. Indeed, the conception does not even enter into the medical field: it is purely political, Utopian, with nothing more than your own blind faith to assure its success ... No, Doctor Axton, it is not in our power to grant your request. Perhaps in a year or two, when you have made further experiments, when you have become willing to share your secret with other members of the profession, it may be possible — It may be possible for us to arrive at a different decision."

Axton drew a deep breath, looked round on the faces. "At least," he said, "I am indebted to you for being so frank, Dr. Meller. It is perfectly obvious to me that your refusal to grant permission is based not so much on your doubts concerning my experiment as on professional jealousy! The facts in this dossier of mine obviously do not interest you enough for you even to mention it. Your sole concern is that I have discovered a secret of glandular surgery which I will not share with other doctors —"

"After all, Doctor Axton —"

"Do you think I care?" Axton shook his head emphatically. "No! If anything, I am deeply grateful that I have been shown the narrow, disgusting bigotry of you gentlemen before being tempted to give away my secret just to secure your permission. You call yourselves men of vision, yet you try to strangle an ideal just because you are not shown the instruments which can make it possible. That I am offering to enrich posterity by giving it a new and wonderful science such as we have never known, that I give assurance that the horrors of the present day will never be repeated, means nothing! The spirit that condemned Louis Pasteur and Lister in the medical world, Alexander Bell with his telephone, Edison with his phonograph, still lives on today … But, in common with those other great pioneers I shall go on to the end in spite of you."

Dr. Meller leaned forward, grim faced. "Do I have to remind you that if you persist in this experiment without sanction from us you will be debarred from practice?"

"No, you don't have to remind me." Axton looked round again and here and there a face turned away before the icy contempt in his gaze. "No; I'm fully aware of the penalties you will exact for my infraction — but I am prepared to face complete boycott, the destruction of my entire practice if need be, rather than forsake my ideal. A day will come when you will see how short-sighted your policy has been." With that he turned and whipped up his briefcase, stalked from the room without another word. He had reached the anteroom and was getting into his coat when he became aware that he was not alone. Prout had followed him, his rubicund face clearly showing his concern.

"Fools!" he breathed angrily. "Blind, jealous fools! They're piqued, you know; that's what's the matter with them."

Axton did not reply. He turned to go, but Prout's sudden grip on his arm gave him pause.

"Just a moment, Axton. I want you to know that *I* fully believe in you. I've seen for myself and … Well, I know you so intimately. I'd really like to help."

"Only you can't, eh?" Axton smiled without warmth. "I quite understand. I cannot expect you to believe in me strongly enough also to risk disbarrment."

"But that's just what I *am* prepared to do!"

Axton stared at him, a puzzled expression crossing his face.

"You ... what?" he asked slowly.

"I mean it! I've seen what you can do. I know that you have imagination enough — foresight if you prefer it — to see what your idea can do for the future of the world and I want to see it through. What do I care for disbarrment? In war they're only too glad to find doctors and be damned to the ethics."

"I should have known," Axton said quietly, patting his friend's plump shoulder. "I should have known. My truest friend always — and at this most needful hour —"

"Just what do you intend to do?" Prout asked, feeling uncomfortable under the eulogy. "If there is any way in which I can help ...?"

"I'm going to get a baby girl from an orphanage or somewhere and use my medical authority to accomplish it," Axton said. "At the moment there is nothing you can usefully do for me, Prout, but be at my laboratory tonight at ten o'clock. By that time, with reasonable luck, I'll be ready for some kind of action."

Prout nodded, gripped the hand held out to him.

"I'll be there. Rely upon it."

CHAPTER III

When Dr. Prout arrived at ten o'clock he found Axton morosely pacing his library, pausing ever and again to meditate. It was a little while before he spoke, and then it was in a grim voice.

"Well, old friend, the Institute works fast! By the time I had reached the first orphanage Dr. Meller had already started the ball rolling. To cut a long story short, I was refused. The reason? Because I am no longer in practice. An outsider! I have spent the rest of today and this evening trying to manage something — without avail."

Prout helped himself to a cigarette. "Then — then what are you going to do? I suppose we couldn't kidnap?"

"Good Lord, no! The whole thing has got to be more or less legal otherwise we'd kill everything right at the start —" Axton broke off and glanced toward the curtained window grimly as there was a sudden explosion not very far off.

"The enemy's a bit nearer this way tonight," he grunted.

"They're over London and suburbs," Prout said. "I had a pretty hectic time getting here in the car as a matter of fact. Sirens sounded just as I left."

Axton became thoughtful again, listening to the distant roar of the London defenses and above it the drone of enemy Mercedes engines. A quiet, contemptuous smile came to his lips.

"Well?" Prout broke the long silence again. "What do we do? There's got to be some way, hasn't there?"

Axton roused himself. "Matter of fact I was just debating the idea of getting some family or other to let me have their child in consideration of a fee, or something on that line — only the more I consider it the less sure I am of success. No family would be so heartless as to release a child to a doctor debarred from practice, I'm afraid … We're up against a damnable problem, Prout, and the more I ponder it the further away I seem to get from a solution —"

Prout started to say something, stopped, looked up sharply at the sudden swishing of a falling bomb. Instinctively he ducked his head. Not a second later there was a monstrous concussion and the library floor swayed under them. Two more explosions followed in quick succession.

"Damned close," Axton said, his grey eyes watching the electrolier swinging in the panelled ceiling. "Perhaps if we went down to my laboratory we'd be safer. Come on." They hurried from the library and across the hall to the basement doorway. Before they could start to descend, however, there was a sudden hammering on the front door, and from the domestic regions came the frantic buzzing of the bell. Axton waited a moment and watched Crawford go quietly across the hall.

The moment the door was open a tin-hatted individual came in. Axton recognized him as Clements, the warden for this particular district.

"Oh, Doctor Axton —" He came hurrying forward urgently. "I need your help. It's most important."

"What's wrong?" Axton asked quietly.

"You heard those bombs come down? One of them got the childrens' boarding-school up on the hill — Miss Travers' place. A ghastly business. There aren't enough doctors to go round in this out of the way spot, so I thought …"

Axton shook his head gravely. "That's bad. But I'm sorry, Clements. I can't help you."

"What on earth do you mean?" Clements stared at him incredulously. "We *need* you! Every doctor we can lay our hands on!"

"I don't doubt it, but it so happens that I am debarred from practice. If it were found that I had done medical work in face of that edict I could lay myself open to imprisonment."

"But Doctor Axton, at a time like this —"

"I'm sorry!" Axton snapped. "If men will fight and destroy they must accept the consequences of their actions. For offering a means of stopping all this bloodshed in the future I have been disavowed by the profession of medicine. Those who are hurt must get on without me."

"This is not like you, Axton," Prout remarked seriously.

"It's how I feel. Why *should* I —"

"Then I must. I'm not debarred — yet."

"Please yourself," Axton shrugged, and stood watching as Prout turned away and accompanied the warden from the hall to the front door. It closed behind them and Crawford returned to the kitchen regions.

"Why should I?" Axton repeated, tightening his lips. "I offer all I have got to the world and I am refused. Yet at the first sign of trouble they come running to me for help. No! I've been too generous …"

He turned impatiently and went down the basement steps, switched on the laboratory lights and thereafter tried to interest himself in a study of his dossier. But all the time his ears were cocked to the sound of falling bombs and the remoter roar of the anti-aircraft barrage. It was easily the worst night attack in this particular district so far.

Presently he lifted his hawklike face to the reinforced ceiling.

"Well, what are you waiting for?" he demanded savagely. "You are not shattering babies' schools and churches just for the fun of it. I don't believe it. You know that somewhere in this area is Doctor James Axton, the man who can smash your wars and beastliness for all future time. Because I wouldn't give you the secret you want to be sure I shan't use it myself … Well, I'm still here —!"

A crash made the delicate instruments grouped about him rattle and tinkle. He looked anxiously round, but nothing was broken.

"Bad shot," he growled, and tugging out his pipe filled the bowl with methodical care. As he drew on the lighted tobacco he dwelt again on the adamant refusal he had given to the warden's plea. Deep down somewhere he knew he had been wrong. In the legal sense quite right, of course — but as a Christian and a man of high moral ideals he had failed miserably. It was not as though adults had been the chief victims. Children. Only that morning he had watched the playground of the boarding-school from his bedroom window and remarked the youngsters' happy obliviousness to the death and horror stalking the land all about them. And now, in the hot murkiness of the September night, an exploding hell of steel and brick —

"God in Heaven, why are men so blind?" he whispered, tossing down his pipe impatiently and getting to his feet. "Here I have the finest discovery ever made — the solution to man's greatest problem, and yet not a single ray of light shines in my path. Why is it so? What is this damnable spirit of prejudice and scorn that would block every grand accomplishment …?"

He turned sharply as the laboratory door clicked. It was Prout who came in, steel helmeted, in his shirt sleeves, his ruddy face covered with grime. He was bearing something almost furtively in his arms.

"Oh — it's you," Axton said. "You're soon back."

"Did all I could, and that was precious little. Seems only a half dozen kids survived that bomb and they're being taken care of now …"

Prout stopped as he saw Axton's sharp eyes studying the bundle he was carrying, a bundle wrapped in a dirt-streaked blanket.

"Prout, what's that?"

For answer he laid the bundle down on the broad top of the operating table. Gently he pulled the blanket aside and revealed a blissfully sleeping child.

"Good God!" Axton gasped.

Prout flexed his arms. "She's pretty heavy, and I judge she is about two years old — perhaps three. Certainly no more. You need a baby girl, so — Well, here you are."

"But man alive, you can't do this! Suppose somebody should find out? Where's she from? — the school?"

"What's left of it," Prout said grimly. "But let me continue — I did all I could, as I've told you. I was getting ready to leave when I heard a throaty snore from somewhere near me. I tracked it to a spot just clear of the main collapse and there, buried under nothing worse than mortar was … her ladyship. Nobody was watching me. In fact I don't think a soul knew she was there. A few minutes longer and the mortar dust might have suffocated her. I got her out, borrowed a blanket — about which nobody asked any questions of course — and … Well, I've left no clue greater than my coat. Not that that matters because everybody knows I was there. I've given her a sleeping draught, by the way, to keep her quiet."

Axton leaned over the child thoughtfully, his eyes studying her closely. She was dressed in night clothes and clearly was quite unaware of the horrors that had blasted around her. Some freakish chance had seen fit to keep her in safety while her schoolmates had been killed or maimed instantly.

"It is said that God watches over the sleeping child and the drunken man," Axton muttered at last. "We can credit the first part, anyway." His questing fingers went to the silken cord round her chubby neck. He tugged at it, found it tangled in her clothing. Finally he ripped forth a label and frowned at it. This at least had not escaped damage.

"'… ray …'" he said, pondering. "See here, Prout. The Christian name is missing and part of the surname. The two ends of the label have been ripped off. 'Ray …' That is all we know." He was silent for a moment, snapping the damaged label between finger and thumb. "How singular!" he exclaimed at last.

"Singular?"

"Only a few moments before you came in I was reviling Fate for not giving me a single ray of light in my path. You bring in a child with that very name — partly the name, anyway. I doubt signs as a rule, but this time …"

"She's a girl, and you need one," Prout said, rather unimaginatively. "What are we waiting for?"

Axton smiled, slowly took off his coat and rolled up his shirt sleeves to the elbow.

"I'm not going to question the why or wherefore of this business, Prout. You found the child and followed your own judgment in bringing her here. I regard that as the direction of Providence. Whom the child really belongs to we don't know, but from her tender years I imagine she is an evacuee, probably from the London area. Normally the children at that school are — or rather were — about ten years of age. Since the war they have taken children of all ages. So out of the unknown comes — 'Ray!' And what a child!" he finished, his voice suddenly keen with medical enthusiasm.

He studied her again, her round, delicately complexioned face, her tangled mass of golden curls. With swift movements, during which she remained dead asleep thanks to the opiate Prout had administered, Axton removed her dusty clothing and switched on the floodlights. He smiled as he surveyed her lissom, perfectly formed little figure.

"Prout," he said at last, "you couldn't have done better!"

"Sheer chance, I assure you. I can't claim any credit."

Axton turned aside and began to wash his hands and forearms thoroughly in antiseptic. After a moment or two he snapped on rubber gloves, then raised the sleeping child gently and laid her on the soft matting Prout put on the table top.

"How long will she sleep?" Axton asked, lowering her down again.

"At least another hour."

"Good! I need no longer than that — but in case she happens to move we'd better strap her down. Can't afford any risks."

Prout nodded and set to work with the straps and buckles. Then he stood waiting, gazing at the naked little form, his mind racing far ahead in speculations. Here on this night, with the thud of bombs still disturbing the quiet, history was being made. He wondered if he would ever live to see the outcome of this strangest of all medical experiments. Normally he would, but with the dangers of war all around him … Then he awoke to alertness again as Axton's brooding, eagle figure turned from selecting his instruments.

They were strange instruments, all of them leading back by electric cables to a little trolley. In it reposed a generator which hummed softly. Prout eyed it in vague astonishment.

"What on earth is it?" he asked, puzzling. "It sounds like electricity, only —"

"It *is* electricity," Axton confirmed, flexing his rubber-gloved fingers.

"What! You mean you have solved the problem of electric surgery? Is this the great discovery you would not confide to the Institute?"

Axton nodded slowly. "Electric surgery of the *nth* degree, old friend, and because you are so loyal to me I don't mind telling you everything about it. To put it briefly, I don't use knives at all: I use rays. Like this …"

He picked up a tubelike instrument and depressed its handle gently between finger and thumb. Prout watched fascinatedly as from it there jetted a hair-thin ray of blinding brilliance, steel-blue in shade. He felt a strong inclination to protest as Axton directed it downwards with a rock-steady hand towards the motionless child. There was something uncanny about the way the ray cleaved through the flesh and left a perfectly clean, bloodless line everywhere it traced.

"You see?" Axton glanced up momentarily and switched off. "This is pure bloodless surgery, the dream of our profession. I've worked on it for twenty years, and now I've wedded it to my gland discoveries. No need for excessive blood loss — instant sealing of the veins, arteries, and capillaries until the job is done."

Prout could only nod: he was too astonished to make any definite comment. Fixedly he watched as Axton resumed his work, saw one after the other of the instruments come into action as, cleavage complete,

Axton turned back a flap of flesh and went to work on the child's internal organs.

Not once did she stir under the painless process, and with jaws clamped lean and tight, his cavernous face thrown into pools of shadow under the arcs, Axton went through all the courses of the operation … Prout saw yellow-tinted beams which prised apart coiled tubes of glands; green, needle-sharp fingers of light which magically knitted up nerve ending with nerve ending. It was the most staggering performance he had ever witnessed with instant death for the child's reward if there was an infinitesimal margin of error. But there was no error — and this in itself was amazing considering the conditions under which the work was being done. For time and again the thud of heavy bombs reverberated through the laboratory, but beyond a sense of occasional swaying no damage was done. For the most part Axton refused utterly to be disturbed.

At the end of an hour he was finished, with nothing to show on the child for his efforts except a rapidly healing scar across the small of her back. He turned her over gently, studied her with brooding eyes from head to foot, then he relaxed and mopped his perspiring face on a towel.

"No wonder you can produce such effects when you never use a knife!" Prout cried at last. "You never touched her with any instrument at all."

"That's the secret," Axton admitted, smiling. "And I don't have to question but that you will keep it safely. These rays of mine — electric vibration would be a better term — are tuned to a millionth of an inch for accuracy. They don't cut the flesh; they vibrate its molecules out of position and leave a clear space. It is not altogether a new idea: many medical scientists have thought of it, but I am the first actually to do it. In brain surgery, I imagine, one could not wish for a better process. However, that is beside the point," he finished, slipping off his gloves. "To me, glandular surgery of this type is just as important."

They were both silent for a moment, then Axton turned and put his instruments away. Presently he returned to the child and became lost in thought.

"She's rather pretty, don't you think?' he murmured, and it seemed a prosaic remark from a man so steeped in the science of anatomy.

"At the moment," Prout agreed, and at that Axton glanced at him sharply.

"At the moment! Good Heavens, man, haven't you even yet rid yourself of the idea that this child must become ugly because of —"

"I wasn't thinking of that. What I mean is, you can never tell how a child will grow up. The pretty ones sometimes become ugly, and the ugly ones — pretty." Prout stopped, hesitated. "You know, Axton, I can quite see how you have managed to alter her gland make-up, utterly turning her, you hope, into a superwoman ... But how can you be sure that at maturity she will do the things you hope for? How can you know that she won't perhaps just become a clever scientist and marry a quite ordinary man, or something?"

"She will never do that," Axton replied in a sober voice. "I have taken chances, I admit. I've made her almost sexless. And I say — *almost*, for I do not consider it within my jurisdiction to decide that she should lead a barren life. She could marry, even have children — probably as strong as herself — but what I have done to her will make her disinclined to do so, I think. You see, this gland experiment is worked out to an ordered plan, one set of glands being altered in exact balance with another. The result, as I see it, will be to give her a strong antipathy towards the opposite sex while yet losing none of her womanly charms and functions ..."

Axton gave a little sigh, clenched his fist and beat it gently on the edge of the operating table.

"I suppose," he said absently, "I have played God! I have delved deeper into the laws of Nature than any man before me and have tried to repattern fundamentals. To this girl out of nowhere I have given a heritage which can never be altered, which will remain with her until death. It is in her hands to, make of her destiny a thing so glorious as to immortalise her, or else to ..." He stopped, playing with a thought. Then he smiled. "There is the other side, but it is not in my power to foresee it. I have simply done my best, as, I know it. If there is a penalty for the thing I have done I am ready and willing to accept it."

He turned, his thoughts back again on the experiment. Carefully he lifted each of the child's eyelids with his thumbs, then lowered them again.

"Be a little while yet," he announced. "The drug you gave her has about worked itself out but there is a slowing up of bodily reactions after what I've done. Bound to be ..."

He paused as though intending to say something more, but instead he listened grimly to the repeated concussions of falling bombs coming ever nearer. Prout's face took on a vague uneasiness.

"Don't like the sound of those bombs, Axton. They're getting much nearer. This place of yours secure against a direct hit?"

"Might be against a small bomb, but with heavy stuff we would not stand the least chance … Remember me telling you that there'd come a time when they'd try to find me?"

"Yes, I remember. But —"

"I have the feeling," Axton muttered, "that it is this very night! That is why I said I was ready to accept whatever penalty there might be for the thing I have done. But my work is finished so my mind is easy. If they don't get me now they will later. I'm a marked man, and I know it. You understand?"

"Yes, even though I don't want to —"

Prout stopped short, struck with genuine alarm as a truly tremendous shock went through the laboratory. This time the floor shifted violently and the more delicate instruments rattled. Several chemical bottles on a top shelf overbalanced and smashed their contents on the bench below.

"We've got to get out," Axton snapped abruptly, his face grim. "Seems they've found the location. Quick — give me a hand!"

He turned swiftly to the operating table and undid the remaining straps, hastily covered the unconscious child in one of his own smocks, then wrapped the blanket round the outside of it. He had hardly done it before both he and Prout were flung off their feet, their ears dinned with sound and their eyes blinded with plaster dust. In the ceiling, reinforced though it was, gaped a rent, gradually widening.

Axton was on his feet again almost immediately, clutching the child to him. He headed for the door, hesitated, then thrust the bundle into Prout's arms.

"Take her for a minute. I want my surgical ray-machine. It took too long for me to build it to let it be destroyed."

Prout nodded, though he was struck with an intense conviction that Axton was making a fatal mistake. His premonition was realised a moment later as the already sagging ceiling broke away under the blast of another bomb. This time there was an inward crumbling of debris from the house above, a monstrous avalanche as beams, timber, and disintegrated concrete came sloughing down. Axton, who had just reached his machine, vanished suddenly in the clouds of dust and hurtling rubble.

"Axton!" Prout screamed.

For a moment he hardly knew what to do. One way lay possible safety for the doorway was still clear. The other way — ? But he turned back, clutching the child to him tenaciously, stumbling and tripping over the stones, thankful for the electric light which was still operating on emergency batteries.

"Axton! Axton! Where the devil are you?"

For a second or two there was no response, then he heard a faint groan somewhere to his left. Laying the child down he went to work with his hands, tugging and clawing frantically until at last he had freed Axton's head and shoulders. That he was badly injured was obvious.

"I'll get help —" Prout gasped.

"No … No, old friend. Not worth it. Get out. More … more bombs may drop yet …"

"But —"

Axton shook his blood-streaked head irritably. "Don't argue! Isn't time. Take the child — somewhere safe." He stopped, seemed to be making a desperate effort to breathe. "Get her — Get her out of the country if you can. Evacuate her. Go with her. You can do … Important you should."

Prout nodded urgently. "Yes — yes, all right. I'll do that. But I can't leave you here like this! I've got to get help!"

"It doesn't matter," Axton whispered, closing his eyes. "I've done my work — and the instruments are destroyed so nobody else can ever use them …" He opened his eyes again and a tired smile flitted over his greying face. "Funny thing, Prout … Just thought of a name for her. I — I noticed when lifting her eyelids that her eyes are a bluish purple — Violet! A lovely shade, Prout. Understand?"

"Yes," Prout muttered, his voice catching. He wondered if Axton was rambling.

"She's — she's a child of science," Axton breathed, his voice hardly audible now. "For my sake call her … Violet Ray."

"Violet Ray." Prout gave a little start. "Of course! Why not?"

"Good! Celebrate it somewhere. Think of me. I —"

Axton stopped, his head dropping back onto the stones.

For a moment Prout could not bring himself to believe the obvious, but the pressure of his fingers upon an artery in Axton's temple convinced him. Life had gone.

Slowly he turned and picked up the child once more, struggled back to the doorway. Even as he reached it a more distant bomb brought down more rubbish with the blast. Somehow he floundered up the steps to discover when he reached the top of them that the house had gone. Instead there was masonry, smouldering with a gathering flame.

In sudden realisation of his peril he hurried on, protecting the child with the blanket until he was free of the debris and in the dew-laden grass. Overhead he could still hear the queer intermittent throbbing of the enemy planes. More bombs swished and the blast nearly lifted him off his feet.

But they were much further away this time. Whether the German airmen knew they had got their target or not he could never hope to learn. Certainly there seemed to be little left in the district which had not been destroyed. Prout's gaze leapt to half a dozen parts where fires were painting the skies.

Suddenly he stopped, all terror going from him. It was one of those moments of impersonal calm, almost exhilarating, such as follow a period of intense strain. Medically, he quite understood his reactions — but at this moment he was a man, not a doctor looking for symptoms, a man swept by visions of a future world. It had suddenly come to him that in his arms he bore the key to the peace of posterity. It was a vast, sobering realisation. It outweighed the vision of destruction, the sight of the searchlights sweeping the skies, the twinkling stars of the bursting antiaircraft shells …

CHAPTER IV

Some three miles to the west of Dr. Axton's crumbled home was the village of Little Beading, an unimportant place on the map but important enough to the firemen and wardens dealing with the hail rained indiscriminately from the sky. At the present moment Vernon Brant, head warden, was finding himself pretty well occupied. With his own particular party of fire fighters he had all his work cut out dealing with falling incendiaries, or when these were less frequent for a while he turned to the task of helping the rescuers to remove the dead or maimed from the shattered cottages.

It was a particularly hellish night, one of the worst Brant could remember. Ever and again as he worked he gazed through the darkness to where he knew his home was situated. There was no sign of any fire, no fatal tell-tale red to signify the destruction of his humble home and possibly the death of his wife Ethel and their three year old daughter, Beatrice. He had left them in the dugout shelter he had devised, their fate otherwise in the hands of Providence. It struck him as odd, the parting remembrance of them that came into his mind — little Beatrice with her doll, looking on the whole filthy business as a thrilling adventure; his wife, calm and dry eyed, with a silk bag full of knitting. She was not a good knitter; she would have scorned it in peace time, but now it was useful to keep her fingers occupied until the steady whistle of the all clear …

And it *was* the all clear! Vernon Brant jerked up his head from the debris over which he had been burrowing. Now, filthy dirty, a grim smile on his lips, he looked up at the sky. It was paling into dawn. Except for the reflection of still burning fires it was curiously peaceful. The wind was fresh and keen with the touch of autumn. There was the smell of new mown hay …

Brant stood erect and took off his tin hat. His eyes moved back to the cottage rubble in which he had been searching. There was nobody there apparently, unless — He turned, smiling with relief, as those for whom he had been searching emerged from their concealed home-made shelter at the far end of the vegetable garden.

"Well, Vernon, one night less to worry about, eh?" commented Pearson, who in normal circumstances was the chief constable.

"Yes, one less," Brant agreed quietly, then as he was about to turn away he paused and stared up the pitted road leading from the village to the next town.

A stumbling figure was approaching, bearing a blanketed bundle in his arms. He was obviously in a bad condition. Blood smeared his face from a head injury and his clothes were in tatters … Immediately Brant hurried forward towards him, and at the same moment the man fell his length, but some latent instinct must have warned him of the value of his charge for when Brant reached him he found the softly crying child still imprisoned in his grip.

The man's eyelids flickered open for a moment as he felt Brant touch him. He spoke in a voice hardly audible.

"Take — take her … Her name's Vi — Violet Ray … I —"

Brant lifted the baby up, raised the blanket from about her face. She rewarded him with a chubby smile and a twinkle of her blue eyes. Brant laughed. He could not help it. It was such a sudden contrast to the hell of the night.

Then there were sounds all around him. The emergency unit had arrived. The fallen man was quickly examined, then the doctor gave a brief signal to the nurse beside him and turned to attend to others. Brant caught his arm.

"Is he —?"

"Yes — dead," the medico acknowledged briefly. "It's a bit of a mystery to me how he kept going as long as he must have done. Something very important on his mind, I expect … Now, if you will excuse me —"

Brant hugged the child to him and watched as the dead man was raised into the ambulance. After a moment or two he went round to the official in charge.

"Was there any identification on that man?" he asked. The official studied the list he had been compiling. "According to the cards in his wallet his name was Prout — a Dr. Alfred Prout. There was a London address."

"I see. This child was with him, but her name isn't the same as his. For the moment I'll take her to my own home where she can be looked after by my wife and I. Once you have traced her relationship to Prout let me know. Her name is Violet Ray, and mine is Vernon Brant. I live at 27 Roseway Terrace, over there."

"Right," the official nodded, and with that Brant turned away and headed across the field which was the short cut to his home.

*

Ethel Brant, pale from a sleepless night of strain, was waiting for her husband in the little kitchen when he arrived. For the moment they exchanged no words. It was an occasion when silent gratitude at still being spared for each other was the only means of expression. Then with a smile Vernon laid his precious bundle on the chesterfield.

"But Vernon — who *is* she?" His wife's slender, understanding hands went immediately to the blanket. She pulled it gently aside then gave a little cry of surprised delight.

"But what a pretty child! Who is she?"

"You are as wise as I am, my dear. I found her in the arms of a poor devil of a doctor who has since died. He must have walked about with her during the night …" Vernon pressed a hand to his forehead for a moment, as though shutting out a memory. "We can take care of her until we know to whom she belongs. She'll be company for Bee, anyway. Where is Bee, anyway?" he broke off sharply. "She isn't —"

"She's asleep," his wife smiled. "Still in the shelter. She had such a disturbed night I thought it best to leave her."

"Of course, dear; you are always thinking for the best. Well, while you study your new toy I'll go and have a shave. Then prepare to meet a hungry husband for breakfast."

He went off with an activity which he was far from feeling, came downstairs again only slightly refreshed to find his wife still studying the child.

"What's her name?" she asked absently.

"The fellow who had her said 'Violet Ray."

"Violet Ray?" Ethel repeated slowly. "Violet Ray? But is that a girl's name? I always thought it meant a lamp of some kind."

45

Vernon laughed. "You mean an ultra violet ray lamp, I suppose. No reason why it shouldn't be a girl's name as well, is there? I shall have to notify the authorities of it and then wait for a claimant."

"That's what I'm afraid of," his wife sighed. "If you don't want to make me unhappy you shouldn't have brought in a child I am liable to lose. Well, this will never do!" she added, looking at the clock. "Work goes on, Jerry or no Jerry, and at this rate you are going to be late for work."

Her husband gave a little yawn as he sat down at the table.

"I wonder," he said slowly, "what a good night's sleep feels like?"

"It will end one day, Vernon. In the meantime it is men like you who are building a better world for millions like her, and our own little one …"

"And women like you," he added seriously, grasping her hand — then as the urgency of the time became evident he turned to his meal …

*

The inquiries concerning Violet Ray brought forth no response from overworked authorities. Apparently every likely avenue was explored in an effort to trace her parentage, without result. Vernon Brant, as the hard, cruel nights of the 1940-41 winter went by and gave place to the lighter evenings of spring, began to become aware of a new responsibility in his hard working life. He had been given an extra daughter from somewhere, a child whose captivating ways were contrasted sharply with the quieter, more introspective ways of Beatrice. There seemed, in fact, to be nothing for it but adoption.

"I see nothing against it," his wife admitted, when he mooted the subject. "In fact, why not? We've become father and mother to her, haven't we?"

"The law doesn't consider that aspect," Vernon replied slowly. "It is more concerned with our financial status. But I don't see that there is anything there open to question. I am a skilled man and the steel business is paying good money these days. No, there is nothing wrong with that angle."

"She and Bee are so happy together," his wife reflected. "They go to the same infant school; they play together … No law would want to destroy that surely?"

Her husband didn't answer. He was gazing before him absently.

"I said no law would want to destroy that," Ethel repeated, and at that he gave a start and looked at her.

"I'm sorry, dear — I was just thinking of the future."

His wife was silent for a moment, studying his strong young face with its clear, purposeful grey eyes. He went on talking earnestly.

"There will come a day, Ethel, when we will have to lay our plans afresh and decide just where we are going to go. Of course a lot of things can happen before this war is over. Though I am thirty-five and a skilled worker I may still be called up. If so, well that is as it should be. But in any event, if I survive until the peace — if *we* survive — I intend to go into steel in a big way."

Ethel went on sewing rhythmically. "What do you mean by a 'big way,' Vernon?"

"I mean make money, and that's the top and bottom of it." His jaw set squarely. "I have a lot of ideas which I can put into practice when things show signs of becoming normal. I want to give Bee and Vi a real chance in life. They are both bright, intelligent kids and they'll be worthy of the best as they get older. They'll never get it in this place unless I make money and a high position in the world. Little Beading is only a village when you've said and done all ..."

He got up from the table and wandered to the window. The early spring evening was fast closing in but it was still possible to see detail outside.

"Ethel," he said quietly, "come here a moment."

When she came to his side he put an arm affectionately about her shoulders.

"What do you see?" he asked gently.

She looked beyond the small fenced enclosure which was doing service as a vegetable garden to the humpy wasteland beyond. Just before the war builders had intended to erect more defilements on this acreage, but they had never got further than the foundations. Rain and general inclemency had done the rest. As a consequence the Brant home was one in the centre of a block, its architecture over twenty years old, its outlook limited to the clayey morass at the back, and beyond it again to the murky backdrop marking the general direction of London.

The front aspect was little better, facing the grey repellent houses opposite. Little Beading was unquestionably old fashioned, useless in fact as far as its industrial contribution to the world was concerned. The nearest heavy industry was twelve miles away — and that had been transferred from a northern headquarters — to which Vernon travelled every day, battling the fog and snow of winter with the same vigour each month.

"I see … squalor," Ethel answered finally. "It's a bit odd that I never noticed it before."

"I am seeing something else," her husband said absently. "I am seeing all these beastly hovels pulled down. I am seeing new, clean workers' homes erected in their place. And this great mass of clay and puddles beyond the garden is a vast, throbbing steelworks. I am at the head of it … That is what I see!"

"You think you can do it?"

"I know I can, providing I'm spared …"

He turned suddenly and gave a little smile.

"Material things first," he said, going across to the little bureau. "I have a letter to get off to the authorities concerning this adoption. Then it will be about siren time, I suppose."

Rather wearily he reached for the pen and ink, and had only just finished writing when the ominous banshee wail spread itself through the gathered darkness outside.

"There we go!" his wife said, gathering up her sewing. "I'll go and join Bee and Vi in the shelter. They should be about asleep by now."

Brant got to his feet and kissed her gently, then with a grim face he turned and reached for his steel helmet …

Once again Vernon Brant survived the deluge of death — and again, and again after that. Then when he felt he could endure it no longer the attacks suddenly ceased …

So preoccupied had he been with his work and wartime duties it came almost as a surprise when he learned that the law had decided to grant him the right of adopting the unknown child. He felt that he had got to get to know her properly: now she was his own, his very own.

Yet there were times when he doubted — particularly a time when at a picnic he had seen her deliberately kill a butterfly. What sort of a nature was behind that?

CHAPTER V

The post-war years brought their problems to the world in general and to the Brant family in particular. In the main, however, it seemed to be a happier, better ordered community than before the catastrophe of 1939.

Vernon Brant took his place in the general scheme of British reconstruction, but at first, so rigid was legislation concerning the use of steel and iron, he could make but little headway. In those years, while the children grew into their early teens, he made little money but kept on hoping. Until gradually the law began to relax its vigilance. The easygoing leisurely days emblematic of real peace and security returned with all the rock-like calm of the Victorian era but with none of its antiquated ideas. Some people stagnated, but Vernon Brant was not one of them. He saw his chance at last to lay the foundations of a steel and iron works. Enterprise, tireless energy, and a keen business sense did the rest …

Over the clayey, derelict land, as the months passed by, there was an ever expanding mass of factory buildings, an increasing array of gates and signs, a constantly multiplying number of heavily smoking chimneys. In what had formerly been Little Beading there appeared workers' homes in place of the cottages — homes which had white fronts, wide suntrap windows, and flat roofs to accommodate one's personal helicopter plane …

In fifteen years Vernon Brant was known as "Steel" Brant from one end of the country to the other. He was known too as a philanthropic employer and a rigid adherent of the square deal. His estate, four miles from the original Little Beading and in the heart of rolling countryside where he and his wife had taken that long gone picnic, was considered to be one of the most beautiful of all the wealthy men of England.

Yes, Vernon Brant had travelled far and prospered, achieved every ideal — save one. He had an adopted daughter of twenty who was fast becoming too much of a handful for him. This day in particular he was resolved to have it out with her. Something had *got* to be done!

Seated in the cabin of his private airplane as he was piloted from an afternoon appointment in London, he went over the causes of his present grievance against Violet Ray Brant. The causes went back a long way too, he found. As far as he could trace, his distrust of his adopted child had begun on that June day when he had seen her so mercilessly exterminate that butterfly. Then, as she had grown older and gone with Beatrice to school, even more startling things had happened.

It brought a grim smile to his face to think of them. There had been the time, for instance, when Bee's life had been made a misery by the bully of her class. For a long time she had stood it in stoic silence — that was Bee's way — until Vi had got to hear of it. Then, with that protectiveness she had always shown Bee, she exacted sudden and violent reprisal. The bully of the class, mysteriously absent from roll call when lessons came round, had been found half unconscious in the mud of the hockey field, her hair cropped so close as to make her half bald and her finger nails cut down to a level which gave her plenty of anguish for weeks afterwards. She never bullied again, but there had been no limit to the invective she had poured forth concerning the yellow skinned girl with the hands of steel whom she had sworn had brought about her misfortunes.

Not that Vi had worried: she had survived everything with complete equanimity and with an almost incredible ease had reached the top of her class. Automatically she had become head girl and her school reports both in the fields of education and athletics had been invariably marked "Distinction". There had never been any question but what she had left the plodding Beatrice far away …

Now they had left schooldays far behind, both of them — and it was now in particular that Vernon Brant felt so incensed. He had planned it that his two girls should enter into families on a par with his own social standing. Bee had shown herself entirely agreeable and, perfectly gowned, had already exercised her youthful charms at several social functions, with — she hoped — potential success.

But of course Vi had followed the dictates of her own intensely individual mind. On the first social occasion she had been deliberately rude to the young men she had encountered; on the second she had walked out in the middle of the proceedings; and last night, the third time, she had been missing at the commencement of the evening, to appear halfway through in filthy overalls, a collection of tools under one arm and a blueprint under the other. When questioned she had become openly insolent.

"Yes, damned insolent!" Vernon Brant breathed, bristling at the memory. "I'll show that young lady exactly what she is going to do for the next three years anyway! Madame Najane's School of Etiquette for Young Ladies — the best that Federated Europe can offer. I'll show *her* …!"

With that his reminiscences and speculations ceased for the plane had just landed on the sweeping expanse of his private parking ground. Clambering out, he strolled across to the house, entering by the broad French windows of the lounge.

He caught Ethel gently to him as she rose from the basket chair to greet him.

"Just as beautiful as ever, my dear, after all these years," he smiled.

"Go on with you!" she reproved, with a little gesture. "Beautiful indeed! I'm getting grey-headed, and so are you. And we're both getting much too stout. All these comforts you keep piling on us will have to stop. We need more exercise."

"We had it — during the war," he said dryly.

"Let's forget that nightmare, Vernon, please. And what do you mean by coming into the house by the French window? Parker will be devastated when he finds he hasn't been able to take your hat in the usual way."

"Oh, damn my hat! Where's the point in owning a place like this if you can't do as you like?"

He tossed it from his hand to the chesterfield, then stood in thought for a moment gazing into the red of the evening.

"Something the matter, dear?" Ethel had stolen to his side and laid a gentle hand on his arm. "Did your London deal go wrong?"

"Good heavens, no! Unless I miss my guess I have a contract which will add several more thousands to my already swollen bank account. No, Ethel, it is not business which is worrying me: it is Vi! She has to be taken in hand."

"Yes, I suppose so." Ethel sat down again and meditated. "I wonder if we have really understood her? She is brilliantly clever; her interests are widespread. And she is so scientific, too! Some of the things she talks about — atoms, electrons, ether waves, and so on — are so utterly beyond me that they make me dizzy. They're beyond you too, aren't they?"

Her husband pursed his lips. Masculine pride forbade that he admit ignorance.

"I admit that she is clever," he said. "I suppose she could win the mathematical chair if she chose ... But that does not give her the right to be insulting."

"If she means it that way. It is not unusual to find that extreme individuality breeds a contempt for others ..." There was silence for a moment, then Vernon gave a little shrug and glanced at his watch.

"Well, I'd better go and freshen up for dinner. I suppose I shall see both her and Bee at the table?"

"As far as I know you will. Bee has gone shopping this afternoon and Vi — Well, I believe she went into the works again."

Vernon frowned. "I wish I could fathom why a girl of her beauty and brains wants to spend so much time in that banging, clattering scorching hell which I've created ... I'll get the facts out of her at dinner time even if it kills me. See if I don't!"

At dinner he found both girls present — Beatrice, dark and quiet, looking more than ever like her mother in her younger days; and Vi, majestic, tawny-skinned, blonde haired, her attention concentrated entirely on her meal. And at the far end of the table Ethel sat patiently waiting for the storm to break, her covert glances moving from one girl to the other and then to her husband sitting in grim, reflective silence ...

Until at last he cleared his throat with unnecessary noise. Beatrice knew that sound from long association and looked up quickly. But Vi took no notice, apparently lost in thought as she progressed with her meal.

"Vi, I'd like your attention for a moment."

"Yes?" She looked up inquiringly and waited. As ever, when there was sharpness in the tone directed towards her a look of challenge came into her blue eyes.

"I have decided to send you away," Vernon proceeded slowly. "To Madame Najane's School of Etiquette for Young Ladies, to be exact. I feel the experience will do you good."

"School of Etiquette — at twenty?" the girl asked, clearly surprised. "What prompted that belated idea? It seems to me that if any education is incomplete you had better have a look at Bee. Her school reports were never more than fifty per cent whereas mine were one hundred."

"Confound your figures, girl!" Vernon said irritably.

"Figures don't lie, father," Vi stated flatly.

"Will you *please* allow me to finish? And let me tell you that you have missed the point, my girl! Since leaving school Bee has conducted herself as any young lady of her station should. She has excellent prospects of marriage into her own set. But you! I'm appalled at the way you behave! If you are not spending your time reading textbooks on science, you are wandering off for days on end where nobody can find you … If not that then you are walking about my steelworks, lying under machines, sitting on the roof girders, talking with the engineers … I *know*! I have heard all about it."

"Is there something in your steelworks I shouldn't see?" she asked dryly.

"Oh, don't be so ridiculous! It's just that it isn't done, Vi! You are the daughter of the owner, not an employee. And I say that it has got to stop!"

The girl was silent, thinking. Vernon compressed his lips in exasperation as he waited for her to say something.

"Anyway, what's it all for?" he burst out. "Why the devil can't you be content with an ordinary life? You have money, security, leisure; I've seen to all those things for you. What more do you want?"

"Power!" she answered quietly. "Power such as has never yet been achieved by my sex — the power to rule, and to destroy if necessary without fear of the consequences."

"Vi!" Ethel was staring at her as though she could not believe her ears. "Vi, do you realise what you're saying?"

"Of course I do!" A tinge of colour crept into the girl's yellow cheeks. "I'm not the kind of girl who can sit and enjoy comfort and wait for some man to come along and give his name to me — such as it's worth. In fact, I detest men. So far as I can make out they are the underlying cause of all humanity's misfortunes and miseries. That there have been great men I freely admit, but in the main …" She broke off with a little shake of her blonde head. "I'll not go into that now, but you might as well know that I can never live the life which is a pleasure to Bee. You see, I'm different — utterly different."

There was silence for a moment. Never had the girl said so much or been so revealing.

"What do you mean — *different*?" Vernon asked at last. "You are a girl of twenty, just as Beatrice is, and all this piffle about power and ambition has got to stop!"

"It can't stop, Father. It's a part of me. I don't know why; it's just there. As for my being different, you all know full well that my physical strength is far above normal for one thing. In your factory, for instance, I have bent steel bars with the greatest of ease, while the toughest of your men hasn't been able to straighten them again. I am immensely strong, and I know it. I'm puzzled by it too, but not enough for me to wish to know the reason. My interest lies in my mental power and how best to turn it to account …" Vi paused and looked round with her intense eyes. "Ever since being a child I have not been interested in everyday things. You must have noticed that."

"We have," Vernon acknowledged grimly, his mind going back down the years.

"I have been pondering scientific things all this time," the girl went on, absently. "I have made myself the mistress of countless scientific arts, both from a thirst for knowledge and from a constant driving urge to do so. Now I know things that can give the control over many, many people …" Vernon rubbed his chin slowly. Back of his mind there was drifting the memory of a crushed butterfly. It had been symbolic, somehow.

"Just an ideal," he said at length, trying to speak lightly. "Just the rather fantastic dream of a young woman. Usually a girl gets lovelorn around your age, but such a condition does not even exist in your intensely practical mind … But it is just as silly, just the same. Why, to even gain the rudiments of this potential power you need money. I happen to know that because I started from comparatively nothing."

"I know, and I watched everything you did so as to have a pattern for my own life. I realised long ago that with my physical strength, scientific knowledge, and money there would be no limit to what I could achieve … So I made money my first concern. That was why I devoted my time to physics on the one hand and spent all my spare time in your steelworks on the other."

"I fail to see how either could give you anything beyond the allowance I provide," Vernon said, mystified.

The girl smiled serenely. "I found out how to do something which has baffled scientists for generations ... how to transmute steel shavings from your factory into an equivalent amount of ... *gold*!"

The silence that dropped was one born of utter incredulity. The girl still smiled, obviously enjoying the sensation she had caused. It was Vernon who spoke first, but it took him all his time to find words.

"But it's utterly impossible! How do you imagine that you, a mere girl of your years, can accomplish something which the cleverest scientists of generations have failed to do?"

A bitter look crossed the girl's face.

"Don't make the mistake, father — especially in these advanced days — of thinking that only men can get a good idea! And my age has nothing to do with it; years don't control the mind. I know how to transmute electrically the atoms of steel into the atomic weight of gold. If that doesn't convince you I'll show you a sample."

She excused herself and left the room. Not a word was spoken until she returned. Then she laid a little oblong bar of gold on the table, perhaps three inches long and one thick.

"Good Lord!" Vernon exclaimed at last, when the gasps of surprise had died down. Picking it up he tossed it in his palm. "Yes, it is gold, definitely."

"I had it valued," the girl said, her arms folded as she looked on. "It is worth two hundred and eighty pounds. The cost to me was about thirty pounds. So that is a clear profit of two hundred and fifty if I choose to sell it."

"But where on earth did you perform this miracle?" Ethel cried.

"That's what I want to know!" her husband snapped. "I'm engineer enough to know that you must have needed a lot of apparatus."

"I have that, in a secret workshop all my own. But that is my own business — and it explains where I vanish to when I am missing for days on end. With the allowance you have made me all these years I got the apparatus together — money which Bee here spent on pleasures and clothes. I work for the future: she does not. That's where we are different ..." Vi took the gold and studied it reflectively. "In other words," she said, in a quiet voice, "I have the means of creating endless wealth. And wealth is the corner-stone of power!"

"Never did I hear of anything to equal it," Beatrice said at last. "I just can't believe it."

"But you are wrong, Vi," Ethel said quietly. "Wealth and power don't mean everything, really. Love of your fellowmen and common humanity are the two ingredients guaranteed to give you a lasting peace."

The girl traced a meaningless pattern on the tablecloth with her finger as she pondered. Finally she said:

"That just happens to be your viewpoint, Mother, that's all. And, without meaning any personal slight, it seems to be the viewpoint of all people who have not the material means — the brains, if you like — to elevate themselves over the masses. I do not say that they are not right, but because those particular virtues do not appeal to me I intend to do things.in my own way."

"To me," Beatrice said, thinking, "this is not altogether a surprise, Vi. I have seen more of you than either mother or father, and many have been the times when I've been either awed or horrified at your brilliance or strength. But, like mother, I think you are getting off on the wrong foot."

"Suppose we let time answer that?" Vi suggested, looking round. "We have no need to squabble about it. I admire and respect your innate womanliness, Bee ... Perhaps it is the one thing about you which I really envy."

"Oh, don't be so ridiculous, girl!" Vernon snorted. "To hear you talk one would think you were an — an outcast or something! You have beauty, charm, and undoubted intelligence. You have youth and money too, even apart from this claim of yours to be able to make gold. — Good Lord, what more *do* you want? I just can't believe that rubbish about power. And another thing, this idea of yours about making endless gold is fundamentally unsound. I am surprised you haven't thought of it. Create too much gold and it loses its value ... So *that* won't get you anywhere!"

"You think I'd be silly enough to overlook that?" she asked in a low voice. "I can assure you that I have mapped out all my life ahead of me, and I have prepared for every contingency."

Both Vernon and his wife began to see that they were faced with a huge problem. There was no time now to speculate on what had driven the girl into these power-lusting channels; no time to wonder what ambitions her unfound parents had had. No — the thing now was to destroy this deadly hydra at the root before it had the chance to flourish into something dangerous to mankind at large. But Vernon did at least feel that he had, if only transiently, got behind the screen of her strange, inscrutable personality. He remembered the butterfly: that had been an act of sheer cruelty for the love of it. Now, on the threshold of adult life, that cruelty was obviously going to rule her whole being unless he, as her foster father, acted ... But it was vitally necessary to act carefully. Arouse her suspicions that he was deliberately frustrating her ideals and anything might happen.

"Vi," he said gravely, looking at her across the table, "I admire your wish to get on in the world, and in many ways that is just as it should be — but I must remind you that you have certain obligations to fulfil to your family — or rather the family which has adopted you — until you reach the age of twenty-one. Until then you are still technically 'a minor.'"

The girl did not reply but an acid smile hung about her well-shaped mouth. Though it made Vernon feel oddly uncomfortable, he went on doggedly.

"I insist that until your majority is attained you obey my wishes. You are still to go to the School of Etiquette and learn something of the social manners necessary in the circles in which we move ... As for these experiments of yours — well, we will see about directing them into the proper channels later on. School will perhaps give you a different outlook to your present one of power-complex. After all, I remember that I too wanted to rule the world when I was eighteen."

"With your ability, Father, and the name you have made for yourself in the commercial world, you could have done it too! Only one thing stopped you — sentiment! However, that is by the way now. If you wish me to go this school I'll go. Maybe I will pick up something of value."

"You are being very wise, my dear," Ethel said gently.

"But," Vi added, looking at each of them in turn, "do not think that I can't see you are doing this because you are ashamed of me! My progressive methods and contempt for men have embarrassed you once or twice, I know. I'm sorry for that, but I can't help the way I'm made."

She got up from the table, then turned as she reached the door.

"When do I go to this — kindergarten?" she asked coldly.

"Tomorrow," Vernon said, clearing his throat. "I have made all the arrangements. The fast plane will take you there. I have told Roberts to pilot you. You will leave at noon, and will reach Madame Najane's about two o'clock."

"I am not incapable!" Vi retorted. "I'll take my own private plane, thank you. I shall need it for relaxation when I reach this seat of learning. Don't worry; I'll leave at noon just as you have ordered … Now, if you don't mind, I'll go up to my room and do a little packing. I'm not trusting it to a servant."

The door closed abruptly. Vernon compressed his lips then sought the eyes of his wife and daughter.

"For a girl of twenty, whom we have brought up in our own way," he said slowly, "she makes me feel infernally embarrassed."

Bee got up suddenly, excused herself and left the room. She hurried swiftly up the broad staircase and along the corridor. In another moment she had entered Vi's bedroom, found her not busy packing but gazing out of the window on to the evening dusk. There was something about her contemplative attitude which gave Bee pause.

"May I — come in?" she enquired hesitantly.

Vi gave a visible start, then turned and gave a colourless smile.

"Why of course, Bee. What is it?"

"I just wanted to tell you that — Well, I think Dad has decided on a very silly course, and I want you to know that I at least don't want to be rid of you. We've been happy together. As for lack of etiquette, I admire it; I wish I could do the same myself sometimes only … Well, I am really Dad's daughter, and you are not. We have a totally different set of hereditary tendencies, which is one thing he seems to overlook …"

"You've always been a nice girl, Bee, with lots of sentiment and feminine charm," Vi said absently, studying her. "As I said before, I envy it at times … Tell me something, quite frankly. What do you hope to get from your future life?"

"Oh, I don't know …" Bee sat on the edge of the bed and reflected. "Since I have social security and a high position, I suppose that marriage and children will be the most I can hope for. I'm not clever like you; I don't know anything about atoms and electricity and such things. All I can wish is that knight errant will turn up one day on his charger and carry me away."

Vi smiled a little. Then she laid a hand on Bee's slim shoulder and looked into her eyes with such steadiness that her gaze dropped shyly.

"Bee, if you'll decide to cast in your lot with me I can give you infinitely more than that. I can give you power, the rulership over our sex, even domination over men. Money and influence such as you have never dreamed of — even a man of your own choosing who dare not refuse your favours. What do you say?"

The silence seemed unusually oppressive to Bee when Vi had finished speaking. She detached herself from the handgrip gently.

"No?" Vi asked quietly.

"No, Vi. I'm — I'm not made that way, I'm afraid. I — I will see you again before you leave, of course and — Excuse me.

Bee left the room swiftly and closed the door. She could not analyse her feelings. For the first time in her long association with Vi she had sensed a repellent hardness in her being which had struck a chill to her heart. Slowly, moodily, she went back downstairs …

And in her room Vi looked out of the window again upon the gradually appearing stars.

"What is to stop me reaching even those?" she whispered. "This is only the beginning of the road. It is for me alone to say where it shall end …"

CHAPTER VI

After lunch the following day Vi was ready for departure. Bee, and her mother and father, were all ready to give her a warm farewell as they went out across the lawn to the private plane — but the girl herself prevented any such effusiveness. She had withdrawn again into that shell of reserve normal to her character.

"Whatever happens, Vi," Vernon said, leaning through the cabin doorway as she sat at the controls, "do not fail to advise us the moment you arrive at Madame Najane's." "You can rely on it," she said briefly, then with hardly a glance added, "Good-bye …"

"Vi, please don't think that we —"

Vernon stopped talking and stood grim-faced as the cabin door shut in his face. In silence with his wife and daughter he watched the machine climb swiftly into the blue sky.

"I wonder," he mused aloud, "if I said too much last night?"

"I think you did," Bee said quietly, and turned back towards the house …

In the meantime Vi kept her machine headed straight for the south coast, until she was sure that she was far enough away from home and steelworks to be right out of sight — then she altered course and turned eastwards, heading swiftly across country on a course which she had already made in secret dozens of times before. She travelled fifty miles, then as below she saw landmarks familiar to her she began to circle gradually, landing a few minutes later.

Just ahead of her was a deserted acreage of land, entirely enclosed with a wire mesh some twelve feet high. In the centre of the enclosure was a series of small, low built, barrack-like huts. In fact they were barracks, left over from the war, and since the peace used variously by builders, forestry experts, and artesian well sinkers, until finally they had been bought by the girl herself for a ridiculously low figure. This had been done by a much older girl whose worldly manner and friendship Vi had deliberately cultivated until, as a personal favour, she had acted as the medium in the transaction. From that moment Vi had dropped her completely, her usefulness outlived. Then, through the months, she had gradually accumulated the machinery necessary for her experiments, carrying a greater part of it herself in her plane ...

Descending from the flyer she looked the enclosure over from end to end, smiling grimly to herself at the sight of the large notice proclaiming the place was private property. Unlocking the high gate, she went over to the first building. Inside it was arranged as a combined room, complete with all necessities from bed and writing bureau to self-generated electric light and cooking appliances. Powered from the same source was a refrigerator, stacked to the ceiling with provisions.

"Home!" the girl breathed, spreading her arms at the freedom of the thought. "Home — where I can think, and plan, and work! No more excuses for my absence, no difficult explanations. The road begins right here ..."

She moved forward again, starting on a tour that led from hut to hut, each building being attached to the other by intercommunicating doors. To Vi it was somehow as though she were viewing it all for the first time.

In one room was her main electrical equipment — a generator, batteries, switchboard, and a bank of fuses. Against a far wall was a television receiver of her own design, and ultra powerful. In another hut were housed the globular electrical devices, anode and cathode, with which she transmuted base metals into other atomic formations. It was a place of marvels, and undoubtedly would have taxed the knowledge of the cleverest electrical engineer.

The third and last hut contained a small printing press and great supplies of paper, together with mechanical cutters. From the hut a rear door led into a long, beetling brick-built annex, which was in truth a small hangar-workshop. The girl had erected it herself, just as she had planned, created, and now finished the steel object lying in its cradle in the centre of the floor. It had been the first thing she had attempted once the hangar had been built — a small, single control flying machine. Experiment and blueprint had proven two things to her — one, that it was capable of attaining heights beyond the atmosphere range; and secondly that it had a speed of eight hundred to a thousand miles an hour, using rocket propulsion and special fuel. Another thing that made it unique was the coating the steel had had, a hard, crystalline substance proof against all forms of energy and heat and therefore invulnerable to the deadly radiations of space experienced in the high altitudes, and also the heat guns used by the sky police when on the track of a fugitive ...

Vi patted the grey bulk with an affection she had never bestowed on a human being. But then, to her mind its streamlined steel was far more worthy of her attention than anything flesh and blood ...

Pensively, she climbed into the control room of the vessel and surveyed it. She was justified in her thrill of pride at the sight of the control board, the twin guns — using disintegrating force instead of the customary heat rays — the small locker, the provision room, the wall bed, the automatic pilot ... In fact her amazing brain had planned a vessel unique in the annals of aviation. It had occurred to her to wonder why on one or two occasions, but she had approached no solution. Had she been aware of the activities of a long dead Dr. Axton she might have understood ...

For perhaps nearly ten minutes she stood thinking, wondering when the need would come to use this ultra powerful machine and planning afresh her strategy for the future. In her own mind she had fully resolved that her life with the Brants was over. It had only come a little sooner than she had expected, that was all ... Ahead of her lay a path to ultimate domination, the vision of men and women everywhere bowing down before her superior strength and mental power.

But if her dreams were grandiose, not to say fantastic, the worries of Beatrice Brant were entirely human and realist. To her as yet unworldly mind Vi was still a sister to be considered and admired, which was one reason why by nightfall she was beset by many anxieties at the absence of any promised news from the girl concerning her safe arrival at Madam Najane's.

"She surely must have got there before this bad weather came up," she asserted, pacing the lounge after evening dinner.

Neither her father nor mother spoke for a moment, but in itself the beat of rain on the windows and the scream of the high autumn win seemed an eloquent testimony as to what might have happened to the girl.

"I'm sure you are worrying yourself over nothing, Bee," her father commented finally. "She must have reached the school long before this storm blew up."

Beatrice turned to him. "In that case let me phone up and find out if she has arrived."

"All right — but I'm sure Vi herself will ring presently if you will only control your fears."

Bee turned to the telephone and pressed the automatic buttons. As she waited for the connection she looked across at her father and said:

"I know Vi better than you do, dad, and it seemed to me that when I talked to her alone last night there was something in her mind which — Oh, hello!" she broke off.

"Is that Madame Najane's school?"

"Yes — yes. Who is that speaking?"

The voice was bluffed with the static created by the storm, which also rendered the face on the vision plate hazy in its outlines ... Quickly Beatrice made the purpose of her call clear, and the dim, crackling reply was not reassuring.

"We have been expecting the young lady since this afternoon. When she did not come we assumed that the storm had caused her to postpone her visit. We —"

There was a sharp click and then silence. Bee rapped sharply on the rest but the line remained dead. Putting the instrument back she turned to her father again.

"Vi has not arrived," she stated quietly.

"Not arrived!" He jumped to his feet quickly and looked across at Ethel in alarm. "But she left here at noon. It wouldn't take her more than an hour to do the trip. What on earth can have happened to her?"

Beatrice was silent for a while, then she seemed to make up her mind.

"If her plane developed engine trouble she would have come down at one of the four emergency stations on the route to the coast," she said finally. "I can't phone them because the storm has broken contact with exchange. There is only one other way to find out ..."

"You don't mean to fly in *this*?" her father exclaimed.

"Why not?" Bee gave a rather anxious smile. "It is simple enough in these days of directional beams, radio pathfinders, and so forth. Besides I have a Grade A pilot's license ... Yes, I'm going to fly. I'm worried as to what Vi may have done."

With that she turned to the door and hurried upstairs to get into her flying togs. In a few minutes she was outside in the swamping rain and battering wind, struggling across the lawn to the plane park. A whiplash of lightning helped her to see where she was going.

She was glad when at length she reached the shelter and comfort of her machine. As far as ordinary flying was concerned she might just as well have been blind, but with the most modern of instruments this was no deterrent.

Switching on the direction map with its numerous radio-controlled illuminated pointers, she studied her intended course for a moment. Then, motor humming strongly, she switched on the helicopter screws and rose vertically into the storm-racked sky.

Soon she was at normal flying height for civilian traffic. Retracting the helicopters she drove the machine forward with ever mounting speed into the teeth of the gale …

Though she had started off confidently enough, she began to feel nervous as her little machine bounced and shook under the impact of the wind. Outside, even when she cut off all internal lights, there was nothing but the dark. All the beacon lights for aircraft were hidden by the density of the storm clouds, a mass of rolling fog with lightning flashing through them with disconcerting frequency and vividness.

Then suddenly the worst happened. It was a contingency which Bee had reckoned with, but which she had felt sure her heavily insulated instrument board would be able to stand. One particularly vicious thrust of lightning threw all her instruments out of commission.

She jabbed frantically at the emergency buttons but they too were out of action. Something very close to panic gripped her as she realised she was alone in the storm and entirely at its mercy … Sitting huddled in her seat she peered into the darkness, or jerked back her head as lightning sent a coruscation of sparks rippling the length of the machine. She knew that she was fighting a losing battle. Without instruments, radio cut off, blown right off her course, what chance had she of — But she went on doggedly, for close on an hour, hoping she would fly out of the storm area for the rain had ceased now and the wind was losing its force …

And abruptly she sailed out of the chaos into wild, savagely beautiful moonlight. Great citadels of bunched storm clouds reared behind her now, their peaks and valleys edged with glittering stars. It was a glorious night now, but — A start of alarm shook her as she gazed below. Land had altogether disappeared! The storm had blown her so far off her course that the shores of Britain or Europe were both out of sight. Instead she was flying at a steady pace with the high wind, at a low altitude over the heaving rollers of the ocean.

Putting in the automatic pilot, she switched on the control light and worked hurriedly to rechart her course by the full moon and stars. It took her about ten minutes to discover that she had travelled in a circle, crossed Britain at high velocity with the sou'wester, and was now careering over the North Sea to nowhere in particular. To rechart her course and turn back for Europe would be simple enough, only … Her startled eyes studied the fuel-gauge. It was nearly empty and in her hurried takeoff she had not bothered to fill the emergency tank either.

Even as she tried to decide what to do there was a tell-tale splutter from the engine, a last spasmodic burst of fire, then it ceased action. Immediately she jumped up and made for the cabin door, but a sudden lurch of the downwardly plunging plane flung her back again. By the time she had recovered her balance it was too late to carry out her intention of baling out. So, stumbling over to the controls, she clung to them desperately as the machine made its final headlong drop —

It struck the sea with a resounding splash and impact, sending water shooting up in a creamy fountain in the moonlight — then it began to sink. Bee found herself forced down in the cabin with water brim full against every window. Only for a moment was she safe then the front port frame cracked under the pressure and the water came swamping inwards. It knocked her flying, plunged her in its depths, choking and struggling for air … With a terrific effort, weighted down by her heavy flying kit, she struck the cabin roof forcibly.

Her lungs were churning knives now at the need for air. She realised that she had only a few seconds between herself and death — a few seconds for clear-headed reasoning. So she swam to the submerged control board and pulled the emergency gun from its clip. With the last ounces of her strength she turned it upward and fired a long thin line of energy through the water towards the cabin roof. It was a rough square she made, and with her final consciousness she drove upward with all the buoyancy of her body. Again her head struck the roof — but the piece sailed away under the impact and she emerged on the surface, drawing in great gulps of cold night air.

For several seconds she could do nothing but recover and thank God that she had escaped. Turning her head she saw the tail of the machine rearing above the surface of the sea and painfully, slowly, climbed on to it. Had she escaped death or had it been just a postponement? That was her worry now. Sky and sea were empty of craft and long exposure in this icy wind might finish what drowning had not.

The thought spurred her to action again. If she could reach the rearing tail there were automatic rockets stored there. She made up her mind immediately and struggled upward towards it. It was hard going for the plane was sinking all the time. Reaching it she encountered another obstacle — how to get into the compartment. All she could do was hammer at the metal covering with her safety knife until she had driven a hole large enough to permit of her hand going through. Struggling and pushing she thrust in her arm up to the shoulder and fished below until at last her fingers closed on two of the rocket flares. Withdrawing them, she looked at the empty sky anxiously.

Ten minutes passed — twenty — and she could feel the plane sinking lower all the time. Then across the darkness of the sky there was a sudden flash ... Rocket exhaust, made by the fast machines which winged the stratosphere. It was so high up that its identification lights were invisible against the background of stars. But for that momentary flash of exhaust, like the streak of a falling star, its presence would never have been revealed at all.

Bee seized one of the rockets, fixed it in the control clamp of the tail, then pressed its detonator button. In a second or two it went off with a gigantic swish into the sky and burst into a blue white glare of discharging magnesium. Bee waited anxiously, loath to use her second rocket in case she might need it for another passing plane ...

For what seemed a long time there was no evidence that her signal had been observed — then to her infinite joy she saw a yellow diamond moving through sky, growing larger. It was the international sign of acknowledgment. So she fired her last rocket to guide the way then waited tensely.

The minutes passed and the plane swept ever lower, until finally it touched the sea and came speeding forward. It was a small, fast stratosphere machine of the type usually used for express mails ... It came alongside and the pilot pushed open his cabin door and switched on the external floodlights.

"Here!" Bee called, waving into the glare. "Get me off quick! I'm sinking!"

"Well, well!" came the pilot's voice. "A new version of rescuing a damsel in distress! It used to be armour and a white charger, and now its airplanes. Never mind, it's the same old thing with a different colour of paint. O.K. — grab!"

A rope whirled out of the light. Pulling on it brought the plane and wreck side by side. With a nimble leap Bee reached the step below the cabin doorway. A strong arm caught her and deposited her into a softly sprung seat facing the control board.

The door closed and the pilot settled down beside her. He was a big, square shouldered fellow with mischievous blue eyes and strongly cut features. His age Bee guessed at about twenty-five. Then, taking off his flying helmet, he released a mop of wavy blond hair and smiled at her.

"Chris Wilson is the name." He extended a brown muscular hand. "Stratosphere pilot flying the Special Australian Package Mail three times a week. Handsome to look at and delightful company. Six feet tall and prone to the charms of brunettes. You were incredibly lucky to have me to rescue you, you know. It might have been anybody — only it was me."

Bee looked at him seriously. "If you don't mind, I am a little weary — too weary to listen to your conceit. I was heading for Europe when the storm brought me down. I shan't continue the journey: all I want is to be landed at the nearest airport."

"Why that?" he asked. "It will be a pleasure to take you right to your home, Miss Brant."

"You know me?" she asked, smiling.

He shrugged leather-jacketed shoulders.

"You take a remarkably good colour photo. I've seen you in the magazines many a time. Rather admired you, as a matter of fact. Funny how Old Man Coincidence has thrown us together, isn't it?"

"Is it?" Bee's voice was cool again.

"My mistake," he said, with a mock shudder. Then, with his hands on the controls he paused and looked at her quizzically. "You are sure you wouldn't like a look at the stratosphere? It's a marvellous sight!"

"Mr. Wilson," she said flatly, "will you please do as I ask and take me home? My parents will be getting anxious."

"All right, home," he agreed, then with that sly smile added, "Via the stratosphere!"

"No!" Bee insisted; then as the rocket motors roared he turned to her again innocently.

"We shall have to go that way to avoid the storm over south England — Hang on! Off we go!"

He made such a noise with the motors that they drowned out her protests. She caught sight of his laughing face, compressed her lips and gave it up. Disdainfully, though she was inwardly conscious of a thrill of pleasure, she turned to look through the window. The moonlit sea was creaming past below, falling ever further away as the fast machine climbed at a steep angle into the sky.

"Ever been in the stratosphere before?" Chris Wilson asked presently.

"No!" she returned shortly.

"You don't know what you've missed." He was quite unabashed. "Up there, there is no air worth mentioning; the machine travels purely by rocket recoil. The stars are hung up like lanterns of God. The sun has a girdle all round him. It's a sight never to be forgotten."

"Sun? At night?" Bee asked dryly.

"I'm talking about the daytime. You'd have to fly away into the void at night to escape the Earth's shadow — There!" he broke off eagerly. "See how the sky is changing, now we are getting really high up?"

Bee didn't answer — not because she wished to maintain her aloof attitude but because the grandeur of things was gripping her. The deep violet of the moonlit night sky was changing with every moment, going through an amazing iridescence of hues, in the midst of which as the atmosphere thinned the stars glittered with ever multiplying frequency — not the winking pallid stars of ground level but hard, brazen points having the steady glow of molten silver.

"Look at it!" Chris Wilson exulted. "It makes you feel like a god up here! See there — that's Andromeda, the great central nebula from which Earth herself was born. Look at it!"

"Yes, it's wonderful," Bee admitted, in a hushed voice, her dark eyes fixed on the misty band of light across infinity.

"And below … the Earth," Chris Wilson murmured. "Seems a bit silly from here, doesn't it?"

Bee looked downwards and gave a start of amazement. All semblance of landscape had vanished. All the contours of sea and land had merged into a common grey where the full moon flooded the landscape. There were clouds, drifting like islands of shadowy cotton wool. And there were stars, too, round the edge of the landscape! It took the girl several seconds to realise that for the first time in her life she was looking on the Earth as a planet.

"How high are we?" she asked breathlessly.

"About one hundred and fifty miles," he answered. "Everything in this cabin is sealed — air, temperature, thermostatic regulation — all the lot. Now, wasn't it worth it?"

Bee nodded silently. Up here in the infinite with the great silent void all round and the motors reduced to a soft purring it was next to impossible to dwell on petty human issues — but she realised that she had to do it.

"You are going a very long way round to my home," she observed.

"I admit it — but surely you agree that it is worth it? However, just to show you that I respect the wishes of such a delightful young lady I'll take you home right away —"

Chris Wilson stopped dead and Bee looked at him curiously. To her surprise all the easy langour had gone from his face and bearing. He had become rigid, staring through the front port with intent eyes. Then almost immediately his fingers were flying over the control board.

The vessel gave a tremendous shudder under the vast strain he suddenly threw upon it.

"What's wrong?" Bee asked, startled, looking through her own window.

He nodded sharply to a distant hazy mass growing rapidly larger right in their path.

"A meteorite," he snapped out. "A massive piece of wandering rock from outer space, half on fire because of the slight air friction at this height. Five miles further up it rains meteors incessantly, at the point where atmosphere ends and space begins. I've encountered things like this before — but never one so big. If that thing hits us we'll smash like an eggshell …"

All the time he had been talking his fingers had been racing over the controls. Bee watched tensely as the machine dived and rocked under the influence of the various rocket tubes propelling it.

"Pity there are no brakes on a stratobus," Chris Wilson panted, and though he tried to say it lightly the girl caught the alarm in his voice and saw the perspiration suddenly gleaming on his forehead. But she did not panic: that would have been the last thing to help the situation. Just the same she could not repress a little gasp of horror at the sight of that glowing mass rushing straight at them from the distance.

Then several things happened simultaneously.

Chris Wilson shifted the controls violently with a last moment effort. The ship dipped with such alarming speed that Bee found herself throw into the control board; then she was lifted bodily out of her seat an hurled right across the cabin as a violent concussion hit the ship. Dazed her head singing from the impact, she stared in front of her. The cabin's ordinary light had been shattered, and to make matters worse this machine was falling with ever increasing speed. Outside the sky was a twirling, dizzy wilderness of stars.

And Chris Wilson? Bee felt cold terror sweep through her as she saw his figure dimly outlined on the floor, a dark streak of what was probably blood across his forehead. Immediately she dived for him and pulled desperately at his broad shoulders.

"Quick! Wake up! We're falling!"

He did not even give the ghost of a movement. Bee got up again and blundered through the gloom to the switchboard — but the maze of complication facing her brought her up short. She turned back to Chris Wilson again and shook him violently, slapped his face and wrists. He moved at last and gave a little groan.

"We're falling!" Bee screamed in his ear. "Out of control! For God's sake wake up and do something!"

"Eh? Huh?" He sat up stiffly in the starshine. "What did you say?"

"We're falling — !"

He jerked himself to his feet and swayed for a moment. Then he lurched to the control board. Bee heard the snapping of switches and muttered expletives — then he stared through the port.

"Too late to save this old tub," he announced grimly. "We'll have to bail out. Here —"

He dived for the cupboard, presumably to get the emergency parachutes — but he was thrown back as the vessel gave an extra violent lurch. He caught Bee to him and held her tightly, covering her head with his great hands and pressing her face against his chest.

"Hang on to me," he panted. "It's too late to bail out now. I've switched on an under-rocket which may cushion our fall, but we're in for the hell of a smack all the same. Hold tight!"

Bee waited through anguishing seconds, then with a sudden stupendous impact the stratoflyer hit water. She had no idea of what happened then. Her last awareness was of being tom from Chris Wilson's grip and hurtling backwards. Her head struck something and she collapsed into a universe of soundless fire.

CHAPTER VII

The radio and newspapers were quick to take up the mysterious disappearance of the Australian Express Package Mail flyer on its return journey and also the simultaneous disappearance of Beatrice Brant, daughter of the famous industrialist. The riddle of why his adopted daughter, Violet Ray Brant, had never arrived at her destination in Europe was also played up, though less prominently.

Letters of sympathy and offers of help poured in to the worried Vernon Brant and his wife. In fact Brant himself was by now at his wits' end to know what to do. Nothing that money could do had been overlooked. Pilots had been employed to scour land and sea over the routes both girls had presumably travelled, but there were no traces of them.

As far as Beatrice was concerned this was not surprising, for after its wild plunge from the stratosphere, Wilson's plane had come down in mid-Atlantic and now lay half submerged with two exhausted figures on its upper works. In fact, Bee was more than exhausted; she was in serious need of medical attention. Unconscious half the time and suffering from exposure, a broken arm and a badly cut head, her chances were none too bright if not given treatment soon. Chris Wilson had done all he could to make her comfortable, spending the rest of his time watching sky and sea assiduously.

Times without number, in the three days and nights they had been floating here, he had seen planes high in the sky — but so high that they had missed the grey speck floating on the surface of the water, and apparently the rockets too which Chris had fired. Now they were exhausted and he was getting pretty close to desperation.

On the fourth day, however, about mid-morning, his roving eyes caught sight of a lone aircraft — and a peculiar one too — floating in a wide circle high above. The sight of it shot him into action and he waved his arms vigorously. Not that it was necessary, for the pilot had obviously seen him. He watched anxiously, then with growing curiosity at the sight of the machine. It was unlike anything he had seen before in his extensive experience, for all the world like a giant flying submarine with portholes lining its sides. Upon the prow he could plainly detect the one word — *Ultra*.

It finally settled smoothly to the ocean surface and then moved forward under the influence of a propeller.

A figure appeared in the airlock — slender, wearing dark blue slacks, blue shirt, and flying jacket. Her hair, golden as the sunshine, was blown away from her clear cut face by the wind, revealing a smooth expanse of highly intelligent forehead. In spite of his weariness Chris Wilson could not resist a quip.

"Well, so the angels have got me already! Where in the world did you come from?"

"I came to find my sister!" It struck Chris that the girl nearly spat the words out. "What is she doing here? I'll warrant she never got into that stratoflyer of her own accord!"

Chris Wilson hesitated, not sure whether to make a hot retort or not, then by the time he had made up his mind to await developments the girl had vaulted lightly to the wreck and was raising Bee's head and shoulders in her arms.

"Bee, it's me — Vi. I'm talking to you! Bee!"

The girl stirred a little and looked up.

"Vi — thank God," she whispered, then her eyes closed again.

Vi slowly stood erect again, her cold eyes fixing Chris Wilson.

"My sister is in pretty bad shape, and she needs medical help right away. I won't ask you now how this all came about, but I will later."

"If you'll only let me get a word in —" But the girl drove Chris into silence with a gesture.

"You'd better come aboard my ship, too," she said, then sweeping aside his effort to help she lifted Bee lightly in her arms, steadied herself, then leapt to the airlock of her own vessel.

When Chris Wilson followed into the control room he found Bee on the wall couch and Vi by the airlock. She slammed it shut and went over to the controls. Silently, with superb ease, the vessel lifted into the air.

"Nice craft," Chris commented, forcing himself to make conversation. "I don't think I ever saw one quite like it."

"That's not surprising," the girl answered shortly. "And at the moment it is my sister and not your useless conversation which is the topic of interest. Do you know a doctor whom we can reach quickly?"

"Sure — there is one at headquarters — Dr. Meller. Just the man."

Vi nodded and said nothing further. Chris Wilson rubbed the back of his head puzzledly and leaned against the control board to study her more closely. Confoundedly good looking, straight nosed, blonde haired, blue eyes — but there was a feline cruelty in the set of that mouth and chin. Evidently strong too, to judge from the easy way she had lifted Bee's not inconsiderable weight. Queer how yellow her skin was, like molten gold —

"If you have finished your scrutiny," she said, staring straight in front of her through the window, "you might take the trouble to direct me to your headquarters. I am not a thought reader."

"Sorry," he apologised, and peered outside. After a moment or two he gave her the course, then relaxed once more.

"I suppose you'll be Violet Ray Brant?" he asked.

"Clever deduction on your part. And you?"

"Oh, I'm Chris Wilson of the Stratosphere Mail. I found your sister's wrecked plane through her firing rockets."

Vi looked up sharply. "You did? Then she wasn't injured when you found her?"

"Well, no … I was taking her home, a flying meteorite hit us, and down we came."

The girl's eyes fixed him.

"Mr. Wilson, you could only have encountered a meteorite by flying at stratosphere heights, and to take my sister home there was no need for that! If she has suffered any serious injury on account of your unwarrantable action I'll see to it that you are held responsible. I'll have you thrown out of the air service entirely!"

"Hang it all, Miss Brant, I was only —"

"I'm not discussing the matter any further at the moment. Please check the course."

Chris obeyed because he did not know what else to do. There was something about this young woman unlike anything he had ever encountered before.

"East," he directed briefly. "Twenty degrees."

So it went on until the great landing fields of the Air Corporation came into sight. The girl brought her machine down gently, and the moment it had halted gathered Bee in her arms and jumped outside.

"This way," Chris Wilson said, directing her to the main building. Presently he held a door open for her and they passed into an enamelled passage and so into a cool, spotless surgery. Still without comment Vi laid Bee down on the divan and then began to pace up and down impatiently after Chris had gone in search of the doctor.

Presently he returned with the medico beside him. Dr. Meller was a white haired man with lean jaws and a rat-trap mouth. For a moment his eyes remained fixed on Vi — so fixed that she gestured, impatiently.

"I am not the patient, doctor — there she is. Please hurry!" With the assurance of a man fully conversant with his profession he refused to be hurried. It seemed indeed almost an effort to him to remove his eyes from Vi, but at last he did so and knelt at Bee's side. His examination was thorough, aided by the highly sensitive instruments he used. Finally he had her arm in a plaster cast and her head bandaged. Then he stood looking at her as the restorative he had administered brought the girl slowly back to consciousness.

"She'll be all right," he said, in response to Vi's questioning look. "Only a cut head and a broken arm — but in these modern days those are only trifles soon healed. In an hour, less even, she will be recovered enough to be taken home."

"Thank you," Vi said quietly. "The Air Corporation will attend to the matter of your fee since it is directly responsible for the accident. In fact it will do more: it will pay a handsome compensation."

Meller's eyes moved from the girl to the discomfited Chris Wilson — then back to the girl again.

"That of course is purely a matter for your own discretion, Miss — er —?"

"I am Violet Ray Brant, and this is my sister Beatrice."

"Indeed!" Meller's eyebrows rose; then he turned abruptly as Bee struggled to rise. "Easy now, Miss Brant — please. Easy!"

"I — What happened?" she asked bewilderedly. "I seem to remember that I —"

"Just a little mishap," Meller hastened to reassure her. "Lie just as you are for the moment while I make a final examination."

Bee looked round dazedly then relaxed again as the medico wheeled up an instrument on rubber wheels. He switched on a cone of lavender tinted light which enveloped the girl from head to foot.

"If you wouldn't mind," he said, glancing at Vi. "Raise her head and shoulders a little."

She nodded and stepped into the beam. Meller made a few technical adjustments to his apparatus and then studied the plate at the back. There was a rather odd look on his face as he switched off, but his words were reassuring enough.

"You have nothing to fear, Miss Brant. Your injuries will heal very rapidly and the cast will be off your arm in three days. You must rest when you get home. I have done all I can for you here."

"You would not mind if she stayed a little longer while Mr. Wilson and I visit the chief of staff, would you?" Vi asked.

"Not at all —"

"Vi!" It was Bee's tired but urgent voice which arrested the girl and Chris Wilson on their way to the door. "Vi, come here a moment ..." Then, when she had complied, "You are not going to report Mr. Wilson, are you?"

"I certainly am. But for him you wouldn't be in this state."

"But for him," Bee said seriously, "I wouldn't even be alive."

Vi waited, obviously for more information. By degrees, Bee got the whole story out.

"So you see," she finished, "It was as much my fault as his. And anyway I wanted to see the stratosphere."

A cold smile spread over Vi's lips.

"But for hearing of your disappearance over the radio and setting out to find you, you would have died as the result of that accident. And the Air Mail is not intended for joy riding! Mr. Wilson deserves, and will get, severe censure. I am going to attend to it now ... Maybe you'll come with me, Mr. Wilson? That is, if you have the courage?"

"I'm not short of that," he retorted, "but it does seem to me that you are making a lot of fuss out of nothing."

"It so happens I do not consider an injured sister nothing," Vi said acidly, and with that turned to the door. Chris followed her, caught up with her in the corridor, and without a word directed her to the Controlling Officer's quarters.

The uniformed official at the desk looked up at Chris Wilson in amazement. Only for a moment did his eyes move to the unusually beautiful girl with him.

"Wilson! When did you get in? We'd about given you up for lost!"

"This young lady rescued me, sir. May I introduce Miss Violet Ray Brant?"

"Delighted, Miss Brant." The official got up and shook hands vigorously. "Brant, eh? Any relation to Vernon Brant?"

"Daughter," she replied briefly.

"Well, well … I'm Captain Thompson, Controller of the air service. I would like —"

"I am here," the girl interrupted, "to lodge a very serious complaint against Wilson here, one that will cost this Corporation a good deal in compensation when I inform my father of the facts."

"Oh?" Thompson's expression changed and he became ominously calm. The girl leaned forward over the desk earnestly.

"The Australia Express plane was lost to you and you were put to the expense of search parties purely because this pilot here had the audacity to take my sister joy riding in the stratosphere against her will. They encountered a brickbat which brought them down in the sea, my sister with a broken arm and head injuries. Those are the facts."

"Well, Wilson, what have you to say?" Thompson snapped.

"I admit it, sir," he answered quietly.

"Very well, the matter will be referred to the Corporation executives for their decision. In the meantime you will consider yourself grounded indefinitely … And thank you, Miss Brant, for your information."

"Purely my duty," she replied, then with a malignant glance at Chris Wilson she went out and closed the door sharply. When she got back to Dr. Meller's surgery she found Beatrice ready for departure, sitting talking to the doctor. She broke off to ask a question as Vi entered.

"What happened, Vi? You didn't —"

"I certainly did, and if the Corporation behaves as it should, it will discharge Wilson from the service … Well, if you are rested enough I will take you home."

Bee nodded slowly and rose to her feet. "Yes, I'm ready. And thank you, Dr. Meller."

"A pleasure," he smiled, holding the door open for them.

Vi leant her arm for Bee as they went down the corridor together. Bee seemed lost in moody thoughts, and only spoke when she found herself confronted with the *Ultra* on the plane park.

"You — you don't mean this is yours, Vi?"

The girl smiled faintly. "I'd forgotten. You've never seen it before, have you? Yes, it's mine — the *Ultra*. The fastest and most invulnerable machine in the world, perhaps."

"But where on earth did you get it? It's finer than any machine I've ever seen — I don't understand."

Vi did not speak until she had settled Bee in the seat beside her at the control board, then when the machine was climbing swiftly into the air she said:

"There are a lot of things about me which you don't understand, Bee — a lot of things which you will never understand. As for this vessel, it is my own design and construction. I built it during the periods I used to vanish from home."

"But for why?" Bee gave a breathless little laugh as she looked round the control room. "It has even got guns! One would think that you built it to escape from something!"

Vi did not speak for a moment or two, and when she did she did not refer to the subject.

"It was good of you, Bee, to try and find me when I didn't turn up at that school. I suppose really that I should have told you that I never intended going, only I never thought you would be much concerned about me."

"But, Vi, why not? We're sisters, aren't we … ? Oh, well, I suppose we're not really, but we love each other as if we were, don't we?"

"I suppose so," Vi admitted, reflecting. "Sometimes, though, I can't help but feel surprised at the importance people seem to attach to love … I often think it is chiefly an excuse to get one's own way; particularly among men." Bee gave her a glance of amazement. "But Vi, what an extraordinary thing to say! You have the oddest ideas; really you have."

"Yes … maybe you're right."

They were silent for a while as the journey continued, then Bee said pensively:

"You were rather rough on my cavalier, Mr. Wilson."

"I was wondering how long you'd be getting around to that. I only did what I considered was right — and you were extremely foolish to go into collusion with him."

"I couldn't help it," Bee sighed, closing her eyes as though to preserve a memory. "He dropped right out of the sky to save me; he even said he was a knight errant. The least I could do to show my gratitude was to visit the stratosphere with him. And besides, I liked his company. He's the first man I ever met whom I felt I could — Well, you know!"

"I'm afraid I don't," Vi said coldly.

Bee opened her eyes crossly. "Oh, you and your science! It's making you cold-blooded, Vi. You'll have to give it up!"

"So I can fall in love with an airman? I think not, Bee ..."

"I wonder," Bee mused, "if I shall ever see him again?"

"Not if I see him first!"

Bee's expression changed. "Now look here, Vi, you haven't the right to rule my life even though you have always taken the lead so far. I can please myself, you know."

"At present," Vi agreed, and there was something about the way she said it which —

Then the Brant private landing field was below them and the topic was dropped. Vi brought the machine down and helped the girl into the house. Immediately they were both the targets of affectionate embrace and reunion.

"But where on earth did you get to?" Vernon Brant cried, as they went in to a hot meal. "Where did you get yourself in such a mess?"

Bee was left to explain in detail, and when she had finished both her father and mother looked across at Vi.

"It is substantially correct," she admitted. "It has meant me coming back home, which I had intended never to do. When I left here for that school I had only one intention — to start my own career in my own way."

"We'll forget the school, Vi," Vernon Brant smiled. "Come back home and live as you want. I should have known better than try to tell a girl of your individuality what to do."

Vi pondered for a moment, then she shook her head. "I'm sorry, Father, but I can't come back here. For one thing I haven't the facilities I need."

"Facilities! What on earth are you talking about?"

"In the career I have set out for myself I have vital need of a workshop, materials, and above all — peace. I can't get it here; you'd ask too many questions, just as you have about that flying machine I've built."

"We'd say nothing," her father said seriously. "Come back; forget these ideals of yours …"

"Sorry, but my mind is made up, and nothing you can say will alter it."

"Now, Vi, look here—"

"I'm tired of this!" she cried abruptly, jumping to her feet and throwing down her serviette. "I only returned at all to bring Bee back. Now that is done I'm finished … I've *got* to go. I can't stand living a conventional life, nor can I stand obeying laws made by a lot of men who don't know what they're talking about anyway …" She paused, looked round even tearfully for a moment. "I'm sorry," she muttered. "It's the way I am, the way I'm made perhaps — but go I must!"

She turned and strode swiftly from the room. Bee relaxed in her chair with a sigh as the door closed.

"I just wonder what is the matter with her?" she muttered, nursing her slinged arm.

"We're in the dark there, Bee," her father answered moodily. "She seems to possess a pronounced wanderlust, and it may be inherited. We can't learn anything about that, I'm afraid. No, I'm afraid all we can hope is that she will return home again — which she will fast enough when she tires of her own company."

CHAPTER VIII

Despite the sweeping brush of progress, so much in evidence after the end of the United Nations' War, despite the rebuilding of London, there had remained one quarter in the city which no amount of law could touch in its entirety, a region outcast from all those except the ones whose bitter circumstances compelled them to seek its sordid shelter and so vanish from the eyes of everyday men and women ...

The Underworld. Located east of London and populated by the scum and down-and-outs of not only Britain, but parts of Federated Europe as well. Every facet of life was represented here, made up of fugitives from the law, refugees from the wrath of outraged European peoples, criminals, murderers, thieves ... There were also exiled politicians, lawyers, artists, actors and actresses, to say nothing of the unnamed of thousands of once big men and women whom revolutionary circumstance had thrown out of the realms of respectable society.

It was into the midst of this labyrinth that there came one night a young woman of no more than twenty, a mere girl indeed, but whose self-possession deflected the most violent invective, whose steel strong hands broke the wrists of those men and women who were inflamed enough to attack her personally. She admitted she was immensely wealthy, and it was the jealousy which this fact created which made her life constantly in danger. Until the outcasts around her realised that she was cruelty itself and as strong as a tigress — then, with the faith of the underdog, they listened to her instead of reviling her. By degrees she won their confidence.

Gradually, as she tightened her hold on them and found out their case histories, she selected men and women and despatched them on different errands, paying them handsomely, assured of their loyalty by very reason of them being fugitives from the law. With new names, forged passports, endless money, they travelled far and wide as her emissaries, but they knew — and she knew — that one word could clamp them behind bars ... So they did as they were told.

But what was this girl — the "Golden Amazon" as they called her — driving at? Why had she sent former financiers and stockbrokers to Europe and different parts of England; why also had she despatched former military strategists to different parts of the country under the guise of commercial travellers; and why had she paid close on a hundred girls a handsome sum to work for her in what was outwardly a clothing factory? Why were the girls sworn to secrecy, on pain of death if they opened their mouths concerning the real nature of their employment? In fact the whole underworld gradually became a gigantic interrogation, with the answer locked in the Golden Amazon's inscrutable brain ...

In twelve months it was autumn again and in that time Violet Ray Brant's connection with the young woman who had failed to reach Madam Najane's School of Etiquette seemed remote. Synthetic gold had bought for her a magnificent suite of offices on the Thames Embankment where, under the trade name of the Plus Clothing Company, she carried on a perfectly legitimate business in the import and export of exclusive gowns and furs, the whole concern, executive and salon, being staffed by men and women recruited normally from the ranks of the everyday ...

But furs and gowns were hardly a merchandise likely to engross the mind of Violet Ray Brant. It made profit enough to please anybody of average taste, but to the girl it was simply a cover for far greater activities. The buyers she had scattered up and down in Britain, the United States, and Federated Europe, were mainly all ex-financiers and brokers empowered by her to deal in the money markets as they saw fit. They had *carte blanche* to cover or corner any particular utility, and invariably, thanks to her unlimited capital and gold reserve, they succeeded in their efforts. If they did not they were simply removed, later to be found and have a verdict of "Found Drowned" applied to them, and be later replaced by somebody more skilful or less careless.

Yes, the ramifications of the Golden Amazon, as she was still popularly called among her underworld intimates, were wide and deep. To her desk in the great private office there came an endless flow of coded cables, stock and share reports, financial news, the whole complicated maze of figures thrown out by the clearing houses of the world's stock-markets every day. She pored over them for hours at a time, knitting together the main threads of her scheme. She did not pretend to understand all the deeper issues of the stock-markets, but her highly mathematical mind was quick to see a chance whenever it occurred — and her agents did the rest. The biggest thrill she got was when this or that Stock Exchange nearly had a panic by the sudden inflow of unexpected capital and gold from sources unknown.

At first, it was the smaller firms which felt the impact of her activities. Her secret agents and endless reserves were an impossible combination to fight, and more than one man or woman found certain ruin straight ahead. Nor was it possible to trace the source of the disaster: the girl had so planned it that activity could never be traced back to her. There were so many channels, so many agents whose very lives depended on them keeping her name secret. So, slowly but with implacable sureness, her financial stranglehold spread like a poison through the whole commercial system of Britain — while in neighbouring countries like the United States and Federated Europe, she went to work to deliberately cut off or buy out the financial branches. Until gradually a peaceful island awoke to the fact that it was becoming financially isolated from the rest of the world, that it was toppling into the midst of the blackest depression and slump in its history …

In time Vernon Brant felt it, though he was beaten when he tried to track down the cause of the clouds gathering on his financial horizon. To his wife and Bee he said little, not wishing to worry them unduly and because in his heart he cherished the hope that things would pick up in time anyway. Besides, he had a special reason for not making Bee unhappy. At the moment she was in the throes of her first romance, for Chris Wilson had proved more than just a passing incident in her life. He had received a sentence of twelve months ground duty for his stratosphere excursion, but the very day after he had been before the executives he had sought Bee out and enquired after her progress. At least that had been his excuse; but both Vernon Brant and his wife noted that it took two hours …

They had raised no awkward objections, however, for both of them had a definite liking for the fellow's frank admission of his faults, and his seemingly never-failing good temper. Of course he was not in the moneyed class and did not pretend to be, but Bee was passionately fond of him and that was all that mattered. The fact that he was in disgrace with the Corporation was tactfully overlooked.

To these two, life held a good deal of promise and both of them were reasonably sure that they could make a good deal out of life together except for one thing. There was a shadow over everything; a shadow which spread right across the country in the form of a slowly tightening industrial depression. It affected even Vernon Brant himself, with a growing seriousness, but never once did he breathe a word to his family of what was in his mind.

He knew — more, he was convinced — that unless a miracle happened very soon he was going to be ruined …

CHAPTER IX

A conference was in progress in the private office of Joseph Millbank, an office situated at the top of the Millbank Building in the centre of London. Millbank himself, short, ox-necked, a living dynamo even at his sixty years of age, was pacing up and down slowly, throwing out remarks now and again and spending the rest of the time listening to his two visitors.

They had been with him for an hour now and represented two formidable names in commerce — Clive Sidcombe, aircraft king, a thin, cruel-faced cadaverous man; and Abner Mainwaring, a research scientist of singular gifts, deceptively jovial looking and as cunning as a fox. Nobody knew exactly the full extent of his activities, not even Millbank, and he knew most things.

"We've got to act, Millbank," Sidcombe insisted. "This Depression has got both you and me into the devil of a mess. A year ago I was running all the major aircraft companies in the country, then suddenly something went wrong. Materials ran short, the Government refused to interest itself in anything outside party politics, and I was forced to close down several factories. Now …" Sidcombe paused and spread his hands helplessly. "Now I'm on the verge of selling my control to a European concern which is benighted enough to think it can salve the wreck."

"That's what gets me," Millbank said bitterly, coming back to the desk. "No concern with a scrap of business acumen would buy a ruined business. That's why I can't help but think that there is somebody behind this Depression who has a monopoly over essential supplies, somebody who is deliberately wrecking the major industries of the country with the idea of reviving them later under one unified control. It's been the ambition of many financiers in the past but lack of endless capital has stopped it. It seems that somebody has that capital — and since we are the victims of it I agree with you that we have to do something, quick."

Millbank paused for a moment and drew on his cigar.

"For that matter, Sidcombe," he went on, "I am as badly hit as you are. Oil is my business and I'll be damned if that isn't cornered too. I've had to close down four of my synthetic fuel plants already and I expect more to follow suit. So far nobody has offered to buy me out, but I'm expecting it any minute."

"Well at least I'm not worrying," Mainwaring said complacently. "My business hasn't been touched because nobody knows a thing about it except you two. Atomic force is a research well worth keeping secret. I have explosives of enough power to tear this country wide open when we decide to fling down the gauntlet to this somnolent Government of ours."

"You can forget your explosives, forget the whole damned atomic force business," Millbank snapped. "You have only progressed at all because Sidcombe and I have financed you. But you'll get nothing more. I sent for you especially to tell you that."

"It may not be so easy as you think, Millbank, to dissociate yourself from the greatest discovery of the age."

"Meaning what —?" Then Millbank looked up impatiently as a clerk knocked and entered. "Well, what is it? I thought I told you I was not to be disturbed."

"I'm sorry, sir, but it is Mr. Brant. He insists on seeing you —"

"Vernon Brant? Why the devil didn't you say so? Show him in. Well, Vernon, how are you?" Millbank extended his hand cordially as Brant entered. "Here, have a chair. Make yourself happy in the midst of dejected company."

Brant smiled faintly round the cigar Millbank lighted for him.

"It's not going to be easy to make myself happy, Millbank, particularly as I have come here to throw some light on our misfortunes, and at the same time throw myself upon your mercy."

The three men looked at him sharply. He looked tired and anxious, they noticed.

"You don't mean you know the reason for the Depression?" Millbank asked quickly.

"Just that … The responsible personage is my daughter, Violet Ray Brant."

"What!" Sidcombe exclaimed, sitting up.

"Surprising, isn't it?" Brant asked colourlessly. "I was not quite sure of it until yesterday. Now I know the truth. She is also the 'Golden Amazon,' that strange, mysterious being who dabbles in high things which has so much caught the public fancy in these troublesome times. The discovery has desolated me, I assure you."

Millbank sat down slowly. "Tell us everything!"

In quiet tones Brant did so, omitting nothing, exaggerating nothing. Millbank drew a deep breath when it was over.

"And what are you going to do about it?" he asked, laying his cigar gently in the ashtray.

"Naturally you will advise the police," Sidcombe said coldly.

"I dare not do that, gentlemen; it would endanger the life of my own daughter, Beatrice. As I have already said, this girl whom I adopted has the whip hand of us —"

"Whip hand be damned!" Millbank snapped. "Be yourself, man! Whoever this girl may be, your adopted daughter or otherwise, she is going to be arrested — and quick! That she happens to belong to you is just your misfortune. I don't have to point out that there is no soul in business, do I?"

Vernon Brant stood up slowly, looked round on the faces.

"I must say that I hardly expected your reaction would be so — violent. I came to you in good faith as a fellow business man, in the belief that together we might work out a plan —"

"Plan!" Millbank echoed. "This is no time for planning! This is the time for law!"

Brant was silent for a moment or two, then he shrugged and picked up his hat and gloves.

"Very well. Maybe I made the mistake of thinking you would respect my confidence. Good morning, gentlemen ..."

He went out with a curious little droop about his shoulders and closed the door quietly. The three men were silent for a moment, rather nonplussed by the disclosure.

Then Millbank slammed his fist on the desk abruptly.

"A twenty year old girl cornering all raw materials, buying up the industry of a country with synthetic gold — ! I just don't believe it. If it happened at all I expect the youngster did it under Brant's orders. He has always been too damned good to be true in his methods — Well?" he snapped, as the same clerk reappeared again.

"There is a Dr. Meller anxious to see you, sir. He says it is most urgent."

"I've no time now. Tell him to call back later —"

"He says it is something about the Depression, sir, and most important."

Millbank glanced at his two companions questioningly and they nodded.

"All right, then — show him in."

The white-haired medico entered slowly, drawing off his gloves and nodding his head in greeting. Without speaking he settled in the chair Millbank proffered.

"Now, doctor, I believe you have something of interest to impart?" Millbank said, trying rather ineffectually to disguise his eagerness.

"Yes … for a price," Meller agreed calmly. He stretched out his legs and surveyed his immaculate shoes. "Unless I am very much mistaken, gentlemen, I am the only man alive who knows exactly what you are up against, who knows the personality at the back of the Depression and incidentally your misfortunes."

"I am afraid you are a little late, doctor," Millbank replied curtly. "We know — and very soon all the world will know — that the responsible person is Violet Ray Brant, or if you prefer it, the Golden Amazon."

Meller sat unmoved by the emphasis Millbank put into his voice.

"You probably are not aware how she comes by her appellation," he said slowly. "There are two reasons for it — her immense physical strength and scientific knowledge. I can assure you, gentlemen, that if you are thinking of calling in the police you had better think again. Police will be powerless against such as her — and I am the one man who knows why. For one hundred thousand pounds I am prepared to sell my information to you."

"Very generous of you, doctor," Millbank said, grim-faced.

"Not only that, I will tell you how to dispose of her!"

"For a hundred thousand pounds!" Millbank exclaimed. "No; I wouldn't even consider it."

Meller shrugged. "Very well. If for a third of that sum between you, you don't wish to rid yourself of this menace, so be it. I chose to come to you, Mr. Millbank, because outside of Vernon Brant — whom I obviously could not approach — you are one of the biggest commercial men. That these two gentlemen happen to be here as well — Mr.

Sidcombe and Mr. Mainwaring, if I recall newspaper photographs correctly — is all to the good. However, if you are not interested —"

"Just a moment," Sidcombe interrupted, as Meller half rose. "Just what do you know? I am willing to pay," he added, glancing at Millbank, "because there is no other way of finding out the truth —"

"How do we know you are genuine, doctor?" Millbank demanded.

"Simple enough. Each of you give me a post-dated cheque for say, two days hence. By that, time, with the plan I have in mind, this girl will be dead … If not — But she will be!"

"I'm not paying a cent," Mainwaring snapped. "I have no need to fear anything from this fantastic woman."

"Perhaps not at the moment," Meller agreed. "Later you may have reason to change your view."

"Why should I worry if these other two are prepared to pay to get her out of the way. I'm not interested, I tell you."

"All right then — that means fifty thousand apiece, gentlemen, post-dated two days ahead."

Sidcombe did not even hesitate, but Millbank did. Then when at last he saw the aircraft man's cheque being handed over he scribbled a cheque on his own account.

"Thank you, gentlemen," Meller said gravely, studying them both then putting them in his wallet. "And now let me explain this matter to you …"

He leaned back in his chair and put his fingertips together.

"We are face to face, gentlemen, with the consummated experiment of a brilliant though somewhat eccentric scientist, whom I knew some twenty years ago — a Dr. James Axton. About twenty years ago I was the President of the Medical Research Institute, and in that capacity I had the power, with other doctors, to permit or veto medical experiments. I'll not go into the details of that, but I'd like to mention the case of this Dr. Axton, who in late 1940 submitted to us a biological dossier of an experiment designed to create a woman of superhuman strength, supreme scientific knowledge, and other exceptional gifts. In plain words — a superwoman! This was to be done by an operation to the gland structure. You are not medical men, but you may know that a scientific control of the glands can entirely alter the physical structure of a human being, man or woman."

The three men nodded silently, absorbed in the revelation.

"Axton wanted a female child on which to experiment," Meller proceeded, his thin lips tightening. "He wanted to produce a woman whom he felt convinced would become a champion of all her sex because of the things he intended doing to her gland structure. For many reasons I refused his request. I realised that if such a child *did* grow to successful maturity she would become a menace to everybody in general, chiefly because no child would be able fully to carry out the wishes of a medical creator but would be governed by her own individual will, and in the case of such a child it would be a ruthless will, un-softened by sentiment and motivated almost exclusively by a lust for power — the quite natural outcome of finding oneself invincible. For another reason I felt sure that such an experiment, unless carried out on a girl-child of more than normal physical resistance, would bring about death, and I didn't want the high tradition of the Institute involved in a possible murder suit. A yet further reason is that for such an experiment there is a terrible price, which will directly involve the hapless victim — the girl herself. For that reason, if for no other, she would be better destroyed now before she has to pay the price for her transcendental superpower …"

"You — you mean that this girl, Brant's foster child, is the grown up child on whom the experiment was conducted?"

"Yes. It was conducted without sanction by us. Axton was infuriated by our veto and vowed to experiment without permission, caring nothing for debarrment or anything else. He had a partner I think, one Dr. Prout — but with the passing of years I've heard nothing of either of them … However, recently there came into my headquarters at the Airport none other than Violet Ray Brant and her foster sister, Beatrice. Beatrice had been slightly injured — but that is inconsequent. What I could not do was take my eyes off the other girl. Yellow skinned, bright eyed, consumed with a tremendous energy. My mind snapped back over the years. Medically, I knew I was looking on the finished product of a gland operation on a major scale. My whole pathological knowledge convinced me of it …

"I made sure, however. I had this girl unconsciously intercept her body in the path of my Y-ray machine. The plate I later developed showed me I was right. Her whole gland structure was right out of conformity with that of an ordinary woman. The coincidence was too obvious to miss ... I knew then whom she really was, and I knew too exactly what fate was in store for her if she lived to experience it before a more violent death overtook her ... Expressed medically, gentlemen, she is a freak of Nature, endowed with an immense, tigerish strength, a brilliant brain, and an almost sexless state of emotion. From a small beginning she will develop, unless stopped, into little less than a fiend, the very opposite of the idea Axton had in mind because as she develops the human restraints will desert her and she will be more and more dominated by the warped gland control which rules her. Until finally —"

"Well?" Millbank asked in a low voice. "Finally?"

"She will burn herself out, literally. She is like a machine running to pieces. Her metabolism is far ahead of normal; her temperature is probably over a hundred. She is consuming energy at a terrific rate which will suddenly expire. Technically, catabolism — the breakdown of cells — will reach its limit and she will be a burned out shell, the ghost of a genius, the wreck of a falsely beautiful woman. A machine, patterned by a scientist to look beautiful, forced by a scientist to be a genius, and likewise condemned by a scientist to ghastly death ... To kill her will do both her, and humanity, a favour."

There was a long, thoughtful silence. Then Millbank carefully knocked the ash from his cigar into the brass tray on his desk.

"Yes, I see now how the police would be unavailing against such a creature. What do you suggest we do? Arrange that she be — er — shot?"

Meller smiled coldly. "Bullets would make but little impression on her unless right to the heart, and even then her vast physical resistance might save her. No, the simplest way to kill a girl like her is to strangle her, cut off the air from her lungs, choke her to death as one would a foul and deadly plant ... But I would add that a task like that should only be undertaken by a man with the strength of an ape and the courage of a lion."

"And for that have we paid a hundred thousand!" Millbank asked sourly.

"Not yet. I can't use the money unless she dies — and I assure you that strangling *will* kill her. With her death the stranglehold over the country will evaporate. But if the attempt fails God knows what will happen. It *must* not fail …" Meller gave a little shrug. "I cannot suggest the person to do the job, only the method. The rest is up to you." That brought another silence, then Sidcombe snapped his fingers abruptly.

"I believe I have a brilliant idea! In fact I think I have the very man to handle this job. He's a thug, pure and simple, an ex-professional wrestler with the hands — of an ape, I think you said, doctor?"

"And the courage of a lion," Meller repeated, gravely.

"Then the Bermondsey Strangler is the man!" Sidcombe declared. "He has both the qualifications and I can soon get into touch with him. The only point will be making sure of getting hold of this girl."

"I'll fix that," Millbank assured him. "I'll give Brant a ring later on, spin him a yarn about us wanting to talk matters over with him and his daughter — Violet Ray — at his home. That will make sure she is in the house. Leave it to me … Now I fancy this calls for a drink! This way, gentlemen."

And he led the way into the private inner office.

CHAPTER X

Vernon Brant did not return home immediately after the meeting with Millbank and his associates. Instead he stopped off at the works and put into effect the decision he had made on the journey up.

In a few short sentences to the workers he announced his intention of relinquishing control of the works — and as he had expected nobody — not even Robinson the chief foreman — seemed much worried. They were too interested in the promises of the Golden Amazon for that. In vain Brant tried to explain that the Amazon was his adopted daughter: if anything it made matters worse. So, grim faced, he returned home and told his wife and Beatrice exactly what he had done.

"In plain language," Beatrice said finally, "you admit that you are ruined — by Vi! Is that it?"

"You could surely have made *some* sort of a show," his wife said.

"How the devil could I? I did everything —"

Brant broke off as Parker, the manservant, appeared in the doorway.

"You are wanted on the telephone, Mr. Brant. Mr. Millbank of London, I believe."

Brant nodded and went out into the hall. It was the voice of the industrialist all right, and his bulldog face was mirrored on the visiplate.

"Oh, hallo, Brant! I've just been discussing affairs a little further with Sidcombe and Mainwaring, and I think — Well, maybe we were a little discourteous when you were over here."

Brant gave an acid smile. "A little!" he echoed.

"You told us a great deal which seems more interesting now we've chewed it over," Millbank went on. "It seems to me that we have got to come to terms with this daughter of yours whether we like it or not."

"Well?" Brant asked quietly. "What's your suggestion?"

"That we meet her. Can you arrange it? We surely ought to be able to arrange a compromise of some kind."

"It's possible," Brant admitted. "Where do we meet? She can be reached at her salon in London —"

"No, no — your home. So much more privacy. If you're agreeable?"

"Very well. I'll get in touch with her and ask her to come over. When exactly do you propose to hold this meeting?"

"We'll be over tomorrow morning first thing. We want to get this thing cleared up. In fact we might even find time to come over later tonight."

"As you wish," Brant agreed. "I'll ask her to come over right away then whenever you come she'll be here. Goodbye."

He replaced the receiver and contacted the Plus Clothing Company. After some preamble he was speaking to the girl herself.

"Do you think, Vi, that you would be prepared to come home to a business conference? Not just on my account, but also to meet Millbank and one or two other big men?"

"I rather thought you told me never to come back," she answered coldly, her face expressionless on the visiplate.

"I meant it," Brant retorted. "That is purely my personal wish. It has nothing to do with business. All I want is a plain 'Yes' or 'No.' if you won't come here we must come to you."

She thought for a moment, then nodded.

"All right, I'll come. I don't think a meeting here would be entirely to my advantage."

"Come over right away then, and stay the night. We might even hold the meeting later on tonight. Millbank hinted at it."

"I'll be there," the girl said briefly, and switched off.

For a while Brant stood thinking, then he turned at the sound of the front door bell. Parker glided into view, to admit a rather untidy individual holding his hat in his hand. "Robinson!" Brant exclaimed in surprise, advancing.

"What brings you here — ? All right, Parker, I'll attend to this."

"I'd like a word with you, sir — private," Robinson said urgently.

"Very well. Come into the study …"

Then when they were both seated the worker looked contrite.

"I suppose I shouldn't have done this, Mr. Brant. I've no right to come to your home like this …" He looked round the well-furnished study with obvious envy.

"Come to the point, man," Brant said irritably. "Frankly, I can't imagine what you want here? I said my last words at the works this afternoon — and so did the rest of you workers. You have decided to follow the lead of my daughter, the Golden Amazon, so I have nothing more to say."

Robinson looked at him strangely. It was hard to judge just what was in his mind.

"We got to thinking about things, sir," he said slowly. "As you noticed, we didn't believe it at first about your daughter — but since then we've seen a newspaper photograph of the Golden Amazon, an old one taken with a sneak camera, and we — or at least I — recognized your daughter, Violet Ray."

"Well?" Brant asked curtly.

"We got to thinking that for all her promises she's probably too young to do much. So we —"

"Prefer the father to the daughter, eh?"

"In a way, sir, that's it. We'd like you to come down to the works right away and see if we can't fix up some kind of compromise."

Brant pondered for a while, then at last he got to his feet.

"Very well, I'll come — but don't expect anything in the way of reinstatements, not until business picks up again, anyway."

"I've got the works car outside, sir."

"Right. Come along."

They went out into the hall together just as Ethel came out of the lounge.

"'Evening, ma'am," Robinson murmured.

"I shall not be long, my dear," Brant smiled at her. "Just going over to the works again. It is possible, though not very likely, that Vi will come here before I return. She will be staying the night at my request. See the arrangements are made, will you? Come, Robinson."

They went out to the car in the evening light and Robinson slipped into the driving seat. With a jerk the car started forward into the gloaming.

Brant sat in silence for a time, his eyes fixed absently on the floodlit tunnel of road ahead of him — then it dawned on him suddenly that they were not taking the main road to the works but a secondary highway which presently crossed the Maylor River.

"Turn back, man!" he ordered abruptly. "We're on the wrong road —"

"No, Mr. Brant, the right one," Robinson replied softly, and the sudden depression of his foot on the accelerator sent the car hurtling forward with dangerous speed. The dusk-hidden hedges streamed by in ribbons of green; the corners twirled crazily as the car skidded and rocked onwards.

For a startled second Brant gazed at the man — then he seized his arm savagely.

"Stop it, you damned fool! Stop this car! Have you gone crazy? We'll reach the river bridge in a few minutes — !"

Brant broke off and snatched his hand away as Robinson suddenly jerked a revolver from his pocket with his free hand, and levelled it.

"Yes — the river bridge!" he breathed. His eyes were wild, his voice punctuated with throaty gasps. "The river bridge that has no parapet! A clear drop of a hundred and fifty feet to deep water! You blasted murderer!" he shouted hoarsely. "Yes, murderer! Thanks to you my wife and I can starve! Thanks to you I can go without a job for the rest of my days, while you live in the lap of luxury! What do you care? You make your pile, then pretend the Depression has killed your business. You put your daughter up to all the tricks with the idea of her securing country-wide control of business … Smart, Mr. Brant, aren't you?"

"You're mad!" Brant panted. "You're crazy! Stop this car —"

"Steady!" Robinson snapped, as Brant made to reach him. "Steady I say! Crazy? Not me! You see, I'm going to cheat the slow death of starvation you planned for me, my wife, and the other workers you kicked out …" He chuckled harshly. "I'm going to kill myself, and do everybody a favour by killing you at the same time! Look!" he broke off gleefully. "There's the bridge!"

Brant stared fixedly for a moment as the great white rise of the bridge lay flooded in the headlamps ahead of them — then he slammed his hand down on Robinson's gun wrist, and with the other seized his neck. He lashed out furiously and fired his gun, the bullet going through the floorboards.

Too late Brant realised that he had made a fatal mistake, for in turning to grapple, Robinson released his hold on the steering wheel just as the car reached the entrance to the bridge. With no guarding rails to either side — the bridge being really a rising road for four lanes of traffic over the river — there was nothing whatever to save the hurtling vehicle. It screamed wildly forward, rubber shrieked on stone, then the car went flying out over the edge into space …

Down and down, the whole hundred and fifty feet, hitting the dark surface of the water with a resounding splash. The car sank immediately, and for the trapped men in the enclosed interior there was no chance of escape as water roared in on them. No chance whatever …

*

It was close on eleven o'clock when Vi's plane settled on the park of the Brant estate. Valise in hand, she hurried across to the house, and Parker admitted her to the lounge. She could tell the moment she entered, that there was something wrong. Ethel Brant, seated in the basket-chair, was drumming her fingers on its arms agitatedly, while Beatrice for her part, pale and anxious was in the act of setting down the telephone.

"Oh — hello," she said indifferently, catching sight of Vi; and her mother did not extend any greeting at all. Instead she got to her feet and began to drive one hand helplessly into the palm of the other.

"Where on earth can he have got to? He seems to — to have totally disappeared!"

Vi came forward slowly. "I hardly expected a welcome, but I still have some legal connection with the family. Maybe I can help. What are you both worrying about?"

Bee swung round and caught the girl's arm imploringly.

"Vi, we never needed help more urgently than we do now. It's dad — he's disappeared somewhere."

"Disappeared! But I came here specially for a business conference with him and several of his associates. Where's he gone? Didn't he say?"

"Three hours ago, maybe more, Robinson from the works called for him. They were going to the works to have a meeting. I've just phoned there for about the seventh time and it seems they have no notions about any meeting, and certainly Robinson and dad haven't turned up."

"You're worrying needlessly," Vi shrugged. "Father knows how to take care of himself."

"I tell you something has happened to him!" Ethel declared hysterically. "I've felt strangely uneasy all day, and now I know the reason why! I —"

She broke off and glanced as the telephone rang in the hall. Vi had reached it before Parker.

"Yes?" she asked quietly, and the face which appeared on the visi-pate was that of a police inspector. She moved a little so that her body blocked the screen from Bee and her mother, now standing behind her anxiously. She only spoke in monosyllables as she listened to the lengthy statement over the wire. When she put the receiver down again her face was set, thoughtful.

"Well, well?" Bee cried. "Don't just stand there! What was it all about? It's news, isn't it? About Dad — ?'

"Yes, it was," Vi admitted, hesitating. "I don't quite know how you are both going to take this — but take it you must. That was the chief of police for the district, Inspector White. An hour ago a freight-boat on the River Maylor hit a piece of wreckage. It turned out to be a fast car which had obviously dropped over the bridge. Two bodies were recovered from the interior and are now in the morgue. One was Robinson, according to the works discharge papers in his pocket, and the other was — Father."

For a second or two there was a deathly silence, then with a low moan, Ethel collapsed her length on the floor.

"Mother!" Bee went down on hands and knees beside her, pulled at her shoulders. "Mother, please! Wake up—!" She looked up desperately, tears in her eyes. "Vi, help me please! What am I to do? She's unconscious …"

Vi stooped and raised Ethel easily in her arms.

"Best thing you can do is get control of yourself," she advised brusquely. "Mother's fainted, that's all; nothing unusual after a shock like that. So get a hold on yourself while I take her up to her room. She'll be all right."

They left the lounge quickly and Bee got slowly to her. feet, dazed, wandered round to the divan and sat on it heavily. Her mind was not yet assimilated to the shock and tears still streamed down her cheeks almost unconsciously. Her father dead — drowned! It just wasn't possible — She looked up abruptly and through the mist of tears saw that Vi was standing in front of her.

"You'd better go up and keep her company, Bee. She is conscious again now, but the shock has hit her pretty hard. I have to go down to police headquarters to identify the body, so I'll call for a doctor on my way back. I shan't be long, should anybody arrive to discuss business."

Bee looked at her fixedly, trying to understand how she could be so calm, so unmoved, as to talk of business at a time like this. It changed her grief into sudden eruptive fury.

"Wait a minute!" she snapped, and Vi paused at the doorway with the kind of expression one might direct to a tiresome child. "Just a moment, Vi! I begin to see now what Chris meant. You're self-centred, heartless. I don't believe you care whether Dad is dead or not! You are — Oh, I hate you! *I hate you!*"

Vi surveyed the distraught face and the tears.

"You're unstrung," she announced quietly. "It doesn't surprise me, though ... Now you go up to Mother and I'll be back as soon as I can."

With that she turned and left the room. Bee stood where she was for a moment or two, then drying her eyes she also left hurriedly and made for the staircase ...

Vi returned in an hour with a doctor. It did not take him long to make his diagnosis, and in the hall the girl was waiting for him.

"Well, Doctor?"

He pondered a moment as he buttoned up his overcoat.

"I am afraid Mrs. Brant has received a severe shock. Her heart is not as strong as it might be, either. However, without undue alarms, she should completely recover. A shocking business altogether about Mr. Brant. You have my profoundest sympathy."

"Thank you," the girl acknowledged and moved to the door with him. "In case of urgency I'll call you at once."

"Yes, do that. Good night."

"Good night."

Vi went back into the lounge slowly, thinking. She had not been alone above five minutes when Bee came in and joined her. She was dry-eyed now, but cold and bitter.

"I'd much prefer it, Vi, if you'd leave," she said sharply, coming right to the point. "Things are bad enough without you here too."

"I have made the funeral arrangements," Vi said, ignoring the request. "The funeral will be three days hence. I also made a few inquiries of the night staff at the works, and it seems that that man Robinson had been behaving very strangely most of the day. Acted as though he were unstrung. In other words, Bee, I don't think Father was drowned because of an accident. It looks as though Robinson deliberately committed suicide and killed father in the doing, probably purposely."

"Dad died because of you, and for no other reason!" Bee blazed back. "But for you there would have been no Depression, no misery, no lack of work to drive a poor devil like Robinson to take his life. He had an imagined grievance against Dad — but Dad died by your hand as surely as if you'd stuck a knife in his heart! Not only has your vicious work struck deep into the very family which raised you, but many other people have been driven to death and crime because of you … I hate you, Vi, hate you now as I would a loathsome disease! You're not my sister really, thank God, so I can disown you. But please, if you have any spark of decency, don't stay on here! I couldn't bear it. Please go!"

Vi shook her blonde head slowly.

"No, Bee, I'm not going. Because my activities have indirectly caused the death of Father is no reason to call me a murderess … You will cool down by tomorrow. You've been under a lot of strain. But I am staying here because I have business to discuss in the morning, Father or no Father … Now I am going to bed, and I am sure it would benefit you to do likewise."

Bee shook her head stubbornly, so with a shrug Vi turned and left the room. Bee only waited a moment or two to give her time to get upstairs, then she hurried into the hall and pressed the telephone buttons urgently.

"Airport?" she asked quickly. "Get me Chris Wilson, will you please?"

There was an interval, then Chris' rather sleepy face appeared on the visiplate.

"Hello, Bee! What's wrong?"

"Chris, I must see you!" The girl kept her voice low, but there was no disguising its urgency. "A terrible thing has happened — Dad has been drowned, and Mother is suffering from the shock. And — and Vi's here now. I'm afraid of her; I really am!"

Chris' face became serious as he saw Bee's distraught features in his own visiplate. He had too much sense to show the shock he himself had experienced at the girl's tragic news. Quiet-voiced, he answered:

"I'll get permission to come right away. Don't worry; I'll soon be with you."

"And come quietly," the girl urged. "I don't want Vi to hear you if it can be helped. No telling what she'd do to me."

"Don't worry. Shadows will be thunderclaps compared to me."

Chris switched off and Bee put down the receiver with a little sigh of relief.

*

In her own room, Vi made no pretence of going to sleep. For that matter she rarely slept above an hour in the night, spending the rest of her time planning or just stretched out, thinking. Fully dressed, she tossed herself on the bed and lay with her hands locked behind her blonde head, gazing at the ceiling. The moon was just rising and cast pale shadows into the room, outlined the rectangle of the big window overlooking the grounds.

After perhaps thirty minutes she heard a faint droning in the night, becoming ever louder — then presently the splutter which her quick ears interpreted as exhaust from an airplane. She sat up suddenly, got off the bed and went to the window, just in time to see the lights of a plane descending to the parking ground at the rear of the estate.

She waited, interested, until a figure appeared in the moonlight, crossing the lawn hurriedly. She knew him in a moment — Chris Wilson. For a moment or two she was in two minds what to do, then she shrugged and made to turn her attention back to the bed — But something caught her eye.

There was a figure moving silently on the next balcony to her own, peering in at the window. She caught the momentary flash of a torch. A big figure, looking for something. Obviously he had climbed the ivy while her attention had been engaged by the airplane. For several moments she watched him, then he turned and slid over the stone balustrade to her own balcony.

She dived for the bed immediately, anxious to see what was about to transpire. Hastily she drew the coverlet over her and assumed a posture of sleep … Presently a torch beam flashed upon her. Immediately she closed her eyes, though she could sense the glare of the light on her face. Then it expired. There followed the click of the window catch and the softest of footfalls on the carpet. Still she made no move, breathing heavily but tensing every nerve —

Something soft caressed her throat, went down over the back of her head, then began to draw tight — She acted! In one violent jerk she tore the silk cord from about her and flung one end upwards. It coiled round the thick neck of the man bending over her, tightened before he even had the chance to realise what was happening.

"Who are you?" the girl breathed in his ear, pulling him down toward her by main strength. "Hurry up! Who are you?"

"Jack — Jackson's the name," he panted hoarsely. "The — the Bermondsey Strangler. I —"

With a sudden swift movement the girl leapt off the bed, spun the man round on his heels by jerking the cord. He staggered clumsily now to reach this creature who had one knee in the small of his back and whose hands of steel were drawing the silk cord tighter with every second.

In a final effort to free himself his hands reached out behind him and clutched her hair. He pulled with every ounce of his brute strength, and unable to shake herself free the girl was flung over his head and crashed on her back on the floor. Immediately, even as she got to her feet, he tore the noose free.

"So that's it!" he panted, peering at her slender form outlined against the window. "Try to do it on me, would you? Well I came 'ere to do a job and I'm going to do it!"

He stood waiting, huge and massive. The overpowering of this slip of a girl looked about the easiest thing he had ever had to attempt. Somewhere in his dumb, brutish nature he even felt a qualm of conscience at the utter defencelessness of his victim. He would have preferred a man, and a strong one —

Suddenly he lunged, but the girl was not there when he arrived. Instead a foot shot out from somewhere and got between his ankles, sent him stumbling towards the window. Out of the gloom a fist drove with pile-driver force and struck him clean in the jaw. Half stunned, he stopped in his rush and rocked. He could not understand it. He had taken the mightiest of punches in the old days, but none had stung like this one. Maybe he was getting soft … He shook his big head to clear it of confusion, then yet another blow landed on him. This time it lifted him right off his feet and dropped him on his back with a crash which shook the room.

Then something sprang at him like a tigress from the shadows. He was pretty sure by now that this woman he had been ordered to strangle could see in the dark. Dully he stirred to meet the menace and scrambled to his feet. A hand closed on his wrist and tightened with fiendish force. He felt the bones crunch and then snap.

With a howl of pain he turned round to fell this female horror with his undamaged hand, but the same instant his free arm was seized and forced backwards with such savagery that it brought tears of anguish to his eyes. Something hit him in the back and toppled him over. It was a knee, crushing into his spine like a vice. Then an arm, strong as iron and supple as silk, clamped under his chin and began to force it upwards. Somehow, in a way he couldn't fathom, a deadly stranglehold had been obtained upon him. The more the arm tightened, the more he felt agony driving into his back and skull.

"Ease up!" he choked, nearly fainting. "I'll — I'll let you alone — Oh, God! Wait ..."

The girl stopped the constriction for a moment, but she did not release her grip.

"Just a few words with you," she murmured. "Who sent you here and for why?"

"It — it was Mr. Sidcombe that sent me. He was told to by Dr. Meller at the airport. I was to strangle you ..."

"How very interesting. And how did you know — or how did Sidcombe know — that I'd be here?"

"He told me he'd arranged it. Something about you being brought here for a business meeting. I — I only had to find your bedroom — Let me go, damn you! You're killing me!"

The girl smiled cruelly in the gloom and tightened her hold a little.

"So Sidcombe, our own little aircraft king, sent you here on the advice of Dr. Meller, did he? And you thought you cold strangle me ... I'll show *you*, Mr. Bermondsey Strangler!"

With a sudden savage movement she tightened her arm to the uttermost. The air cut off from the hapless man's lungs. He struggled and fought wildly, nearly dislodging her, but that arm seemed immovable. He felt his head bursting ... Darkness roared in upon him.

Slowly, as he relaxed, the girl removed her arm. She peered at him in the moonlight, then felt his heart. It was still beating turgidly. Reaching out for the silk cord she tied it round his neck, then using a coat-anger in the loop she tourniquetted it to the limit. In that position she knotted it three times, withdrew the coat-hanger, then surveyed the empurpled face with its protruding tongue.

Abruptly there was a hammering on the door and the voice of Beatrice. The girl gave a start, then she got to her feet and switched on the light, flung the door wide. Bee came in slowly, still fully dressed, and stared at the figure on the carpet. Then she jerked her face away in sudden revulsion. Vi gave a crooked smile and flung back the tumbled hair from before her face.

"You're looking on the lout who was sent here to strangle me," she said, breathing stormily. "Sidcombe sent him, and there is not the least doubt that Father was in on it since he arranged I should be here to be strangled! So, in getting drowned he only got his deserts."

"You're lying!" Bee screamed, hysterically. "It's all a mass of lies! Dad would never have done that — You're a murderess! *A murderess!* And this proves it!"

"There is a pronounced difference between murder and self-defence, Bee. It was him or me … I'm sorry if the scuffle disturbed you or mother only —"

Vi broke off abruptly as the figure of Chris Wilson appeared.

"You, eh?" she said laconically. "I'm not surprised, you know; I saw you arrive. Incidentally, what the devil do you want here, anyway?"

"I came to give Bee what assistance I can. With her father dead and her mother ill, I consider it my duty. Besides." Chris added pointedly, "I didn't feel comfortable with her left in the house with you."

Vi's bitter smile was something very close to a snarl. It occurred to Chris for a moment, with a shock of alarm, that he had never seen a human face so closely resembling that of a dangerous animal. Every time he saw this strange girl she seemed crueller, more alien …

"What's been going on here?" he demanded. "We heard the noise down in the lounge and Bee insisted on seeing what was happening. Who is this man, anyway?"

"Supposing I told you?" Vi snapped. "What do you propose doing about it? Calling the police?"

"By rights I should!"

"Then don't! This is my own affair, and any police who come here will only make it the worse for you and Bee and won't benefit me in the least. Just get out, both of you, and forget all about it. Or better still, see if darling Mother has been disturbed. I'll take care of this!" The girl kicked the corpse contemptuously.

"What are you going to do with him?" Chris Wilson demanded.

"Return him to Sidcombe with my compliments, together with a warning that Sidcombe had better watch himself from now on!"

With that Vi stooped, seized the corpse by the coat collar, then yanked it to its feet with sudden effort. Carrying the heavy body in her arms, she went out on to the balcony and tossed the corpse to the grounds below. Then she crossed the room again to the doorway, the eyes of Chris and Bee following her with incredulous horror.

"Never did I know a girl to be so unspeakably horrible," Bee whispered, then with a little shudder she buried her face suddenly on Chris Wilson's shoulder.

Vi turned in the doorway. "It was his life or mine, Bee. I told you that before, and since Father — your own dear father — was partly responsible for the whole effort, I don't see what you have to yell about. In this life, you'll find out that men will do anything to gain their ends. I'm probably the first woman who works the same way, and before I'm finished I'll take full toll for this night's work!"

Then she was gone. In a few minutes she had gone round the house to the sprawling body. Seizing it by the collar again she dragged it bumpingly through the shrubbery and to the parking ground where her flying machine was standing beside Chris Wilson's. Without ceremony she jerked the corpse upward and dumped it in a back seat of the cabin. Then starting up the engine she set her machine climbing swiftly into the pale dawn sky and settled herself to study out her course ... Some fifteen minutes later she was over a deserted country estate — Sidcombe's home. Quickly she brought the machine to rest just outside the grounds.

It took her only a few minutes to reach the front door of the residence. She jabbed the doorbell steadily and consistently until at last the door opened and a begowned manservant peered into the dawn light.

"What is the meaning of —?" Then he stopped as he saw a gun in the girl's slender hand.

"Inside!" she ordered. "I want a word with your master, and I don't want announcing either. Where is he? Still asleep, I suppose?"

"No, miss — he's gone away," the man answered nervously, his eyes moving from the gun to her face.

"Gone away! Where to?"

"He left home about midnight, with the family. He said he would spend the night in London, then all of them would take the eight-thirty plane this morning to Europe from London Central Airport."

Vi glanced at her watch. It was just on six-thirty now. For a moment or so she thought swiftly. It would be too risky to try and nab Sidcombe or any of his family at the London airport. But there might be another way — Her eyes flashed back to the manservant.

"Did he say why he was leaving?"

"He only said that sudden urgent business made it necessary for him and the family to go to Europe."

"I'll bet he did," the girl said bitterly, then as she put her gun away she added, "If you're lying I'll come back and settle with you — and Sidcombe."

With that she turned away, but she knew the man had not been lying. There had been no reason for him to do so; no ready idea to save his master. Ideas did not come that quickly so early in the morning anyway. One thing was at least plainly obvious to the girl. Sidcombe was taking no chances in case his plan to kill her had misfired …

Reaching her air machine again she scrambled back into her seat, lifted the flyer to the level of the housetop, then switched on the helicopter screws to keep it stationary. Glancing outside she saw that she was poised at about twelve feet above one of the house's skylights. She smiled to herself, then tearing a leaf from her control board pad she wrote a few words — *With the Compliments of the Golden Amazon.*

Getting up again, she went to the back of the cabin, pinned the note on the dead Strangler's coat lapel, then dragged him along the floor to where a trap lay in front of the control board. Opening it she peered below. Picking the Strangler up again by belt and coat collar she leaned forward with him dangling in space just below the trap …

Abruptly she released him. His flailing body went hurtling through the window amidst a shower of glass, making a din which awoke the dawn echoes …

In one bound the girl was back at the control board. Retracting the helicopters she gave a burst to the machine which made its rivets creak. In a few seconds the Sidcombe residence was whirling away into the mists of the morning.

"Meller!" Vi breathed, her eyes narrowed as she sat at the switches. "I can get him at the Airport, and if not there I can get his address. I have an overdue account with that gentleman!"

CHAPTER XI

When Vi reached the local airport she was informed that Meller's duties did not commence for another two hours, and that even then there was no guarantee of his arrival since he was a voluntary worker. Without any difficulty she obtained his home address and directions for reaching it in the quickest way. To her satisfaction it was only ten minutes in her machine, and turned out to be a big house in its own grounds. Obviously the doctor was wealthy, giving his services to the Air Corporation purely to keep his hand in.

Vi surveyed the place for a while from above, then finally brought the *Ultra* down on the landing ground adjoining the estate. Leaving it there with the controls locked, she went to the front door of the residence and rang steadily. Presently a manservant appeared and looked out upon her curiously.

"Is the doctor in?" she asked quickly. "It is most urgent."

"Have you an appointment, miss?"

"No, but you can give Dr. Meller my name — Violet Ray Brant. I am sure he will see me."

"Just a moment, please." The man vanished, to return after a while and hold the door open wide. "Yes, Dr. Meller will spare you a few minutes, miss, though he is very busy in his laboratory. Please come this way …"

He led the way through a broad hall resplendent with brass plaques and polished armour to a door at the far end. Opening it, it gave ingress on to a roomy, fully equipped laboratory well lighted by numerous skylights.

"Miss Brant, sir," the manservant announced, and then retired.

Vi stood waiting impatiently, gazing over the wilderness of instruments, bottles, and medical paraphernalia — then she turned as the whitehaired Meller came into view along the central aisle between the benches. There was a curious half smile on his cadaverous visage.

"Good morning, Miss Brant. What can I do for you?" She studied him for a long moment without speaking. It was a deadly stare, and Meller, hardened though he was, felt an irresistible urge to look away. But he didn't. By a sheer effort he kept his eyes steadily fixed on those icy blue ones; then at last the girl spoke.

"Why did you tell Sidcombe to send the Bermondsey Strangler to kill me?"

"My dear young lady, I didn't." Meller relaxed against the bench.

"Don't lie to me, Meller! I know all the facts."

"Well, that's very interesting. Since you know so much, I freely admit that I told Sidcombe you needed killing. That you are still alive is costing me a good deal of money."

"It will probably cost you your life. That you suggested I be murdered seems to me sufficient reason for me murdering you."

"There are laws against murder," Meller said calmly.

"That didn't stop you!"

"I didn't intend to commit the deed. Nobody could have proved that the suggestion was mine. It was purely verbal." The girl moved forward slowly, her fists clenched. Then within an inch of the unmoved doctor she stopped.

"I suppose I would be a fool to do it myself," she said slowly. "But don't think for a moment that I won't retaliate. You can't do that sort of thing to me and get away with it."

"Do as you wish," Meller shrugged. "I have no intention of being afraid of a freak, especially one who will drop dead at any moment."

The girl looked at him quickly. "What did you say?"

"My dear young lady, I am an experienced doctor, and I know exactly what the cause of your pathological condition is, the reason for your immense strength and vibrant personality. You see, you are not a normal woman but a scientific experiment, the living proof of a zealous doctor's dream twenty years ago."

The anger died out of the girl's eyes and was replaced by curiosity.

"Tell me more; I'm interested."

"Come over here," Meller said, and leading the way to a little office adjoining the laboratory he drew up two chairs, then leaned forward earnestly. Without any hesitation — indeed with a brutal, vindictive frankness — he told the girl everything he had told the industrialists. Then with a cold smile on his lips he concluded:

"Medically, there can only be one end to a human being designed as you are — or to any living organism which consumes more energy that it can ever replace — and that end is early death and, before that, an incredibly abrupt old age with the failure of every faculty."

"Why?" the girl asked in a faraway voice, staring at him.

"Because you are telescoping a hundred years of normal bodily expenditure into a third of the time. Excessive metabolism is the technical term. The huge energy you consume, mentally and physically, cannot possibly be replaced. Suddenly you will come to an end of your resources and become old, burned out — dead! A death that will be painful too, encompassing as it will the failure of the body and the mind … But the world will be the better for it."

The girl was silent for a long moment, then she said slowly:

"I don't believe it."

"I can prove it if you're interested," he answered. "Let me take your temperature."

Since she said nothing he picked up a clinical thermometer from the rack behind him and thrust it under her tongue. When he withdrew it he studied it and smiled, then handed it over. It registered one hundred and six.

"That would kill a normal being," Meller said dryly. "To you it is normal to have an energy warmth eight degrees higher than average. There's your proof …"

The girl flung the thermometer savagely on the floor and got to her feet.

"You're not frightening me, Dr. Meller. If I find myself faced with any ailment, I'll think up a counteractive quickly enough."

Meller said nothing, but his eyes studied her, seemed to infuriate her all the more.

"So a man did this to me, did he?" she breathed. "He set out to meddle with my life and changed me from a normal woman into … into what I am. I'll make his sex pay for that. I'll show them no mercy. None! You hear, Dr. Meller?"

"For my part, Miss Brant — or Golden Amazon if you prefer it — I don't intend to let you live a moment longer than I can help. And for three reasons — You are a menace to society because your power-complex disease is progressive; I want to save you from the anguishing end to which you are inevitably doomed; and last of all I don't intend to let a big amount of money slide out of my hands too easily …"

"You're very frank, Dr. Meller. And you don't suppose I shall attempt nothing against you, do you?"

"Not at all; but I'm prepared to match wits against you any day. Since I failed to stop you being made into a superwoman twenty years ago I am prepared to attempt it now …"

The girl smiled crookedly. "You're going to have a big job on, Dr. Meller — and you will have to travel a little too because I am leaving for Federated Europe right away. Find me there, if you can! And take care I don't find you first! … Good morning."

The manservant showed her out of the house and she hurried over to her machine. Once in the air again she headed southwards — to Europe — until she was out of sight of Meller's, home; then she turned back on her tracks and flew at top speed to the Brant estate, landing fifteen minutes later.

Hurrying into the lounge she found Chris Wilson there. He did no say a word, just stood by the window and looked at her, but she was not blind to the hostility in his eyes. "Where's Bee?" she asked curtly.

"With her mother." Then Chris snapped, "Well, did you get rid of that thug you killed?"

"I did." Vi swung to the telephone and pressed the buttons quickly. A uniformed official appeared on the plate. Chris stood listening to the girl's voice just inside the hall.

"London Central Airport? Will you let me have your passenger list for the eight-thirty Europe express?"

"Certainly, madam," squawked the receiver, and there was a pause; then the voice resumed rapidly:

"Thank you," the girl said finally, and replaced the receiver. Returning into the lounge thoughtfully she gave a little laugh. "Lord, what fools men are! I set a trap for that idiot Dr. Meller and he walks right into it!"

Chris gave a start. "Dr. Meller — from the airport? What on earth has he got to do with it?"

"Nothing beyond the fact that it was at his suggestion that the Bermondsey Strangler was sent to kill me!" The girl's eyes flamed. "When I went to see him he told me that he would spare no effort to kill me. I promised him the same thing in return. And I rather think I am going to win," she finished slowly. "You see, I told him I was leaving for Europe right away. The only immediate plane he can book for Europe is the eight-thirty from London Central Airport. In fifteen minutes it will be off. The airport has just assured me that he has booked a reservation,"

"But why are you so anxious to get him on the plane to Europe?" Chris demanded, mystified.

"Because I can kill two birds with one stone. Sidcombe, who sent the Bermondsey Strangler on Meller's advice, will be aboard that plane as well, with his family. I was intending to kill him anyway. That is why I wanted to get Meller at the same time if possible. And I've done it!"

"With only fifteen minutes to get aboard that plane?"' Chris asked. "You've slipped, haven't you? In any case I don't see how you could kill two men on a busy air liner without being detected."

"That is simple, Mr. Wilson. I shall destroy the liner!"

He stared aghast. "You'll do what?"

"Destroy the liner!"

"But you can't kill hundreds of innocent people just to get at Sidcombe and Miller! It's — it's inhuman!"

The girl gave a crooked smile. "I am not going to, Mr. Wilson — *you* are going to do it! I have been waiting for a long time to get you out of my way, to break your association with Beatrice. You are an interference. I repeat, you will destroy that liner — and I don't want any arguments!" she snapped, whipping her revolver out of her pocket. "Go on — move! Out to my machine on the park there!"

"But, Bee —"

"She'll be all right. She's old enough to look after herself without your manly solace — Hurry up, can't you!"

Chris looked at her determined face, then at the gun. It was no time to throw his life away in trying conclusions with her, especially as he had good reason to know her superhuman strength. Turning, he went out ahead of her across the lawn to the *Ultra*. The girl followed him into the control cabin and seated herself half askew at the switches so that she could watch his every move as he stood by the side port.

The controls moved under her fingers and the machine climbed upward rapidly for some fifteen minutes. The girl seemed satisfied then for she turned in her seat and peered downwards … An infinite distance below, perhaps ninety or a hundred miles, lay the bulk of England sprawled in the morning sunshine — and far to the eastward the misty expanses of Federated Europe. Between the two glinted the North Sea and English Channel. After a time, Vi busied herself with a telescopic device which viewed the air directly under the *Ultra* by means of lenses in the floor. For fifteen minutes she steadily searched the ocean of sky, cruising the vessel round in wide circles — then finally she glanced up with gleaming eyes.

"There's the eight-thirty liner! About fifty miles below!"

To see it with the naked eye in the vast vault was impossible, but its position was perfectly recorded on the instruments. In a moment the girl had the ship plunging down at sickening speed in a roaring power-dive.

Chris, a trained pilot, kept his position in spite of the wild, sweeping lunges. The landscape below twisted and turned in circles, came nearer and nearer. Air screamed past the thick, streamlined hull — Then all of a sudden the girl flattened the machine out and the huge bulk of the Europe express hove into view pursuing its soundless, majestic way high over the gathered clouds of morning.

With a swift movement the girl put in the automatic pilot then turned to one of the twin guns. Chris moved towards her but her revolver whipped up and stayed him.

"Better not!" she advised grimly.

He hesitated, looked back through the window. For a moment he had a vision of countless faces looking out of the windows of the sun lounges. The passengers were evidently interested in this strange visitant of the skyways, so unlike anything they had ever seen before —

Then Vi depressed the gun levers. Sheer astonishment held Chris as he beheld the frightful power of the instrument she was using. Whole pieces of the liner's armour-plate went sailing into space, liquefying even as they moved and then dropping in molten splashes to the distances below.

The faces had abruptly vanished. There was instead a confusion of movement as panic must have gripped the passengers. Then, as the girl still held the levers down, Chris saw the giant machine's windows go stoving in; more plates buckled and warped. The whole mass of the air liner slewed round in a half circle and began to lose altitude.

"What the devil — !"

Chris let out a hoarse gasp, then horrified at his impotence so far he dived for the girl and knocked her revolver flying before she had the chance to use it. Seizing her round the neck from behind he dragged her backwards by main strength, sent her flying across the cabin with one sweep of his powerful arm. She stumbled and half fell, then got to her feet again with flaming eyes.

"Surprised, eh?" Chris grated out. "First time a man ever kicked you around a bit, isn't it?"

She did not answer but he could see she was tensing herself for a sudden spring. And abruptly it came. He jumped to one side, but in that she had anticipated him, for she landed with her hands locked at his throat. Immediately his own hands came up, closed with all their power round her forearms. For a moment or two it was sheer muscular effort on the part of both of them, then the girl's foot suddenly hooked out and caught Chris a stinging blow on the ankle. He gasped with the pain, lost his balance for a moment and went reeling against the gun-seat. Like steel grapples the girl's fingers dug into his neck, forcing him down. He realised breathing was becoming more and more of an effort …

Desperately he gathered himself for a supreme effort, tightened his fingers to the limit of their strength, dug his thumbs into her wrists. He felt her relax slightly under the pressure as he purposely crushed on to the main tendons of her hands. Then he shoved with every ounce of his strength. The girl's hold gave way and she fell backwards: in a second her wrists were imprisoned behind her in a ju-jitsu hold and she found it impossible to break free. Smiling triumphantly Chris snatched the leather belt from about her waist and buckled it securely round her arms. Then he pushed her into the chair by the wall.

"Well?" she blazed at him, tossing her tumbled hair from before her eyes. "How far does this get you?"

"Quite a long way towards finishing you, I hope. I ought to congratulate myself for being the first man to beat the muscles of the much vaunted Golden Amazon."

Rather to his surprise she relaxed.

"I haven't finished with you yet," she said quietly.

"As far as I'm concerned, Miss Brant, you've finished with everything! I'm going to do now what I should have done at first when I found you up to your little tricks — hand you over to the police. Or else to a psychopathic hospital. One thing I am sure of, and that is that you are not sane."

She said nothing to that and he watched her narrowly. From the movements of her shoulders he judged correctly that she was exerting every ounce of her strength to break the tough belt holding her. Then again she relaxed, smiling crookedly, her eyes upon him.

He turned away from her at length and looked through the window. The remains of the shattered air liner had vanished now and the *Ultra* was swinging round in aimless circles. Then he gave a start. Out of the gulf below machines were shooting upwards — two, six, eight ... Stratosphere planes bearing the insignia of the Sky Police. Vi saw them too through her own window and from her expression it would have been hard to judge exactly what was passing through her mind.

"Saves me a bit of trouble, eh?" Chris asked, regarding her. "My own department is after you for that liner attack, and I'm not surprised."

Still she did not speak, but her eyes wandered to the control board and then to the ceiling. Vaguely he wondered why. There was nothing wrong with the lighting, anyway. Inside the *Ultra* the yellow bulbs gave a greater brilliance than daylight itself. What, then, had passed through her mind ... ?

By now the police machines had gathered into a group and were patrolling alongside the *Ultra*. The "Stop!" signal flashed from the prow of the leader.

Chris turned to the radio equipment and switched it on. He was just about to tell the police that the *Ultra* was out of control when the girl suddenly vomited from her chair. He wheeled, astounded, had just time to see broken ends of belt still fastened to her wrists — then a fist of steel sent him flying into the wall. He caught his head a fiendish crack and reeled dizzily. The girl's venomous yellow face seemed to dance in a mist as she rained blows upon him, drove him to the floor by the sheer violence of her attack.

Half stunned, his head singing with pain, he saw her scramble over to the switchboard and move a control. For some reason the lights in the *Ultra* changed to a bright blue, neutralising every other colour. Then the girl got the machine on to an even keel and slowed it down.

"Come aboard!" she invited, switching on the radio; and a vague amazement stirred Chris at her request. But he still could not think straight, and the blue light worried him, too. It had turned the glitter of the ship's appointments to sapphire reflections.

Vi closed the switch which controlled the airlock, and presently it opened to admit five air police in flying kit. They took off their oxygen helmets then looked about them, their guns at the ready.

"Thank God you came!" Vi cried in sudden thankfulness, and her voice was so human for once, so divested of its usual cold authority, that Chris could only gaze in wonderment.

"What's been going on here?" demanded the leading officer harshly. "You're both under arrest. This machine made a deliberate attack on the Europe air express. We were advised of it by radio and —"

"It wasn't us — it was him!" Vi interrupted, pointing to the bemused Chris as he stood by the wall.

"Him!" The officer twirled, then gave a start. "Why, it's Chris Wilson —"

"He kidnapped me!" the girl went on urgently. "He forced me into this machine at the point of a revolver … Here it is," she added, picking up her own weapon from the control board bench. "That is the solemn truth, officer. He told me that he had been wanting revenge on the Air Corporation for some time because of them grounding him and that this machine of mine was just the thing. When I refused he — Well, he did as I've told you. I think he had some idea of blaming the attack on me, but after all why should *I* want to destroy an air liner?"

The girl looked round with wide, innocent blue eyes.

"She's lying!" Chris yelled. "She's doing it deliberately —"

"I'm *not* lying!" Vi shouted hysterically. "He must have lost his reason or something for a while. You know who he is well enough. He even tied me down in that chair, but I broke free. See, here are the straps still fastened on my wrists."

The officer's eyes narrowed at Chris.

"This is a serious charge, Wilson, and I'll have to take you in. Kidnapping and destroying an air liner, to say nothing of stealing this young lady's plane for the job. You've the hell of a lot of explaining to do —"

"Oh, don't be a damned idiot!" Chris exploded. "Can't you see the whole thing is a trick? This girl is Violet Ray Brant — the Golden Amazon! She did it!"

"Even if that be true, which I don't believe, the Golden Amazon is not criminally inclined. She's just a — politician — and anyway her skin's yellow. I know what the Amazon looks like; most people do."

"How the devil do you expect her to look yellow in a blue light? We all look alike in this tint. I tell you that she is the Amazon and that she knocked me out —"

"She knocked *you* out!" The officer glanced at her slender form then smiled without warmth. "You're getting deeper every minute. Blue Light be damned!" he snapped. "What kind of fools do you think we are?"

"Oh, take him in charge!" the girl said bitterly. "I'll prefer charges against him later."

The officer signalled to his men.

"Look here," Chris said urgently, and the handcuffs clicked on his wrists, "why can't you give me a proper chance? Take this into a proper light and see her for yourself. She is the Amazon I tell you —"

"And I tell you that it doesn't matter a damn if she is! We have no authority to do anything with her. You're coming with us! Go on — get moving!" The officer glanced at the girl. "You will be notified when you are needed for evidence. Otherwise you are free to go."

"Thank you, officer, so much," she said quietly.

The officer turned back to Chris. "Here, put on this spare oxygen helmet — and hurry up! Go on — out!"

Slowly Chris obeyed, crossed over to the police ship moored alongside. Vi watched until the planes were speeding off into distance, then she closed the airlocks and with a triumphant smile set about the return journey home.

It had been a good morning's work, she decided. Sidcombe and Dr. Meller accounted for, and Chris Wilson — the one danger she had sensed all along — safely out of harm's way for some time to come … She laughed gently to herself.

*

When Vi got back to the Brant home she found Beatrice pacing up and down the lounge agitatedly. The moment Vi entered she came to a stop and swung round to face her.

"Where's Chris? Where did you take him? I saw you leaving the house and going over to your machine. I know Chris would never have done it of his own accord, especially without even saying good-bye."

Vi glanced at her watch. "I think the problem will best be solved by listening to the ten o'clock news bulletin. Shall we switch on …?"

She pressed the button of the instrument and waited without speaking while the morning concert played itself out. The vision of the orchestra on the scanning screen vanished and was replaced by a fade-in of the station announcer. After rambling through the preliminaries of the station's wavelength and so forth he came suddenly to the point.

"A very serious happening is reported this morning in connection with the eight-thirty European express air liner from London Central Airport. The liner was attacked without the least provocation by a machine of unusual design and bearing the name of *Ultra*. The liner was totally wrecked and very few of the passengers who bailed out have survived. Sky police caught the attacker who has proven to be Christopher Wilson, ex-pilot and now a maintenance man of Section B of the Air Corporation. Sentenced to ground duty for twelve months nearly a year ago for flagrant breach of regulations, it can only be stated at this moment that he deliberately planned the attack as an act of revenge. A further charge has been lodged against him — that of kidnapping. It was discovered that he had aboard the *Ultra* the owner of the machine — Miss Violet Ray Brant, whose father's death in tragic circumstances we reported last night. Miss Brant stated that Wilson had kidnapped her and stolen her machine. She was allowed to return home after Wilson had been taken into custody. A full list of the names of missing passengers will be broadcast the moment it is complete …"

There was a pause. Beatrice had come to the teleradio and was staring at it fixedly. Then her eyes rose to Vi's coldly smiling face.

"Lies!" Bee whispered, her voice quivering. "Nothing else but beastly lies! You deliberately got Chris out of the way!"

"I did — because he was in mine. I —"

Vi paused as the station announcer started speaking again.

"A matter of immediate interest has just come to our notice, ladies and gentlemen. We have in the studio now a very well-known personage in the world of commerce who has a statement to broadcast to the country — Mr. Joseph Millbank."

"Millbank!" Vi echoed, startled. "What does he want?"

She stared at the screen in smouldering fury as the industrialist's face, dogged and grim, merged into view …

"What I have to say is vitally important," he began, "and I beg of everybody in the land, wherever my voice may reach, to take serious heed of my words … There is abroad in our midst a strange and deadly character, a woman of youth, of rare beauty, of vast strength, a woman who is heartless and cruel, who destroys whatever blocks her ultimate aim — which I am convinced is nothing less than the domination of this country. She is a dictatress in the making … This woman is the mysterious personage whom some of you have called 'The Golden Amazon'. During last night she murdered, in cold blood, one of the foremen employed by Clive Sidcombe, the aircraft manufacturer, who it is feared now has lost his life in that destroyed air liner …

"I have learned, as have the police, that the strangled body of the foreman was thrown through a skylight of Sidcombe's home this morning, presumably from an aircraft, with a note affixed to it saying — 'With the Compliments of the Golden Amazon.' The Sidcombe manservant also reports being held up at the point of a gun by an amber skinned girl earlier in the morning — undoubtedly the Golden Amazon … And now the real sensation! I have positive proof that the Golden Amazon is actually Violet Ray Brant, whose story of being kidnapped aboard her own ship is nothing but a tissue of lies. I say that she destroyed that air liner and deliberately shifted the blame to Chris Wilson, who in a statement has sworn this was so … I demand that the law take action and arrest her! She is behind the Depression, the misery of this country today. Scientific skill allied to brutal lust to domination has always spelt ill for mankind, and it is here against us once more. Allowed to remain free, this girl may —"

Vi switched off abruptly, her eyes glittering.

"The filthy, lying swine!" she muttered. "He conveniently forgets to mention that the foreman — the Bermondsey Strangler — was sent to murder me in the first place … Foreman indeed! I'll get Millbank for this! I'll kill him! You see if I don't!"

"As long as you get out of here and never come back you can take your own road to the gallows!" Bee retorted harshly. "The law knows the truth now and it will very soon catch up with you!"

"Law! What do I care for law? The strongest power is the law, and *I* am that! And don't get the idea, Bee, that you are going to stay here and tell all you know to the police! You are coming with me. I have everything prepared for just such an emergency as this —"

"But I can't!" Bee cried. "I have Mother to look after. She is ill —"

"A professional nurse can do that. I'll attend to it."

Vi turned away to the telephone in the hall. In a few minutes she had summoned a professional nurse, got her promise to be present within ten minutes. With a gratified smile she put the receiver back and turned —

Bee was facing her, her face set resolutely, an automatic gripped tightly in her right hand. In a voice that trembled noticeably she spoke.

"You didn't think I'd ever have the nerve to hold a gun, did you? Well I'm doing it! It was Dad's gun, and now it's mine. You going to the phone gave me the chance I needed to get it out of the bureau drawer —"

Bee stopped and came closer until the gun muzzle was prodding lightly into Vi's breast above her heart.

"I've stood as much as I can, Vi! My father dead, my mother ill, Chris in prison, and you threatening to take me away — No, I won't do it! I'll kill you first and the law can decide if I did wrong. You and your vile, murderous scheming! Oh, to God that I'd seen all this long ago, as others did. You are staying here until the police arrive, and if you don't I'll put all the bullets in this gun through that black heart of yours — *Oh*!"

She broke off with an involuntary cry as Vi's right hand came up like the head of a snake and struck her right across the face. It was a vicious, stinging blow which sent her reeling against the panelled wall of the hall, the gun dropping out of her hand. Half stunned she fell her length and shook her head dazedly.

"Now get up!" Vi's hand reached under her arm and jolted her to her feet again. Bee lurched dizzily, then rubbed her tingling cheek.

"And don't get any silly ideas like that again," Vi added, pocketing the gun, "because if you do I may not be so lenient. And another thing, if you dare say a word or give so much as a signal to the nurse when she comes I'll give your arm a twitch that will make you faint. Understand?"

Bee gave a little tug but failed to dislodge the iron grip prisoning her upper arm.

"What in God's name has come over you, Vi!' she whispered, half in unbelief. "That you could do such things to me, of all people —"

"Oh, stop such sentimental tosh! To me you are just a unit from now on, and a very close unit because you know so much ... Now get into that lounge and keep your mouth shut when the nurse comes ..."

She released her hold suddenly, but put such a spin on it that Bee went flying into the room beyond and sprawled helplessly on the carpet. Weakly, trembling in every limb, she crawled to the divan and lay there, trying vainly to quell the tears rushing to her eyes.

"For God's sake stop snivelling!" Vi snapped at length — then she turned as the front door bell rang. She forestalled Parker and got to the doorway first to admit the nurse. Bee realised a short conversation took place, then the nurse hurried upstairs and Vi came back into the lounge.

"If you've finished bawling we'll be on our way," she announced brutally. "You don't have to worry about mother. She will be all right, and the nurse will explain to her that you have been called away ... Now come!"

"I won't, Vi! I won't! The shock of this might even kill mother! She'll know you are back of it —"

Vi's eyes narrowed to agate points. "I said — come!" she repeated.

Bee stared at her for a moment, then very slowly she got to her feet and pushed away her damp handkerchief. Because she was mortally afraid to do anything else, she accompanied Vi outside to the *Ultra*. Once inside the machine she stood for a moment looking back longingly at the house, then the cabin door slammed in her face and Vi pushed her roughly into the second seat beside the control board.

"No time for your mooning," she said briefly. "And keep quiet while I'm piloting ..."

So Bee sat motionless, biting her lip to check more tears as the machine rose swiftly into the morning sunshine. Silence was easy enough for her for she was in no mood for conversation, but her curiosity was gradually aroused as she found Vi piloting the machine swiftly over deserted countryside until at length, after a study of landmarks, she brought the machine down and to a halt. Now they were at ground level Beatrice could descry an assortment of huts surrounded by a high wired enclosure. From above the camouflage had been absolute.

"Yes, it's mine," Vi said dryly, seeing Bee's eyes looking round in wonder. "To the eye, just a group of huts — an experimental chicken farm, if the sign there is to be believed. A year ago I had a few machines and experimental quarters in those huts, but now it is very different. I have had the time, the money, and the machines to dig underground ... My workshops are deep, protected by steel trapdoors and thick concrete roofs. You will see — and you will be surprised. Just stay in your seat and watch."

She touched a lever. Massive wheels suddenly sprung from the *Ultra's* belly and lifted her two feet from the ground. The vessel moved slowly towards the enclosure gates, which abruptly opened.

"Photoelectric cell lock," Vi said briefly. "When we have passed through the area of the beam the gates will close again."

They did — and the *Ultra* taxied forward to a concrete runway facing a rising hill of ground. Another door opened, or rather an enormously thick steel slide shot up. When the *Ultra* passed beyond it, it snapped down and there was sudden darkness until the machine's headlamps revealed a downwardly slanting tunnel ahead. It terminated in a small steel enclosure and here Vi brought the machine to a stop.

Opening the cabin airlock, she jumped outside and lifted Bee down beside her. They left the little underground hangar by a small emergency door and so stepped into a perfectly equipped office of tremendous size. It was brilliantly lighted, as though with snow white flame, and apart from the usual business furnishings there was one wall full of television instruments and screens, and the opposite one was in truth a gigantic window through which there was a view of a workshop extending into an infinite distance.

"The illumination is cold light," Vi said, and she failed to suppress the thrill of pride in her voice. "A blaze of brilliance and not a scrap of heat. Scientists have searched for that in vain all these years — but I found it! In itself it is worth a fortune, but what is the good of that when I have an endless supply of money ..."

Bee advanced wonderingly, everything else forgotten for the moment. In the workshop beyond — it reminded her of a gigantic underground railway station in area — there were only women, she noticed, all in overalls of dark blue colour and working on —

"Planes!" Bee exclaimed, with a start of surprise. "They are planes, aren't they?"

Vi was standing beside her, gazing broodingly on to the industry.

"Yes, Bee, they're planes. These girls I have working for me are all skilled mechanics, specially trained by instructors I have employed for the purpose. But all of them — instructors and girls — are fugitives from the law! They are handpicked from the lowest reaches of life. Girls who want revenge on the law and society and who know they can get it through me. Therefore they are willing workers and loyal. There are fifty of them working for me here, picked with great care by my agents, and in the steel filing cabinets here are full records of their case-histories. Yet another fifty are elsewhere in the country receiving instruction on how to become pilots of these flying machines ..."

"But — why?" Bee asked blankly.

Vi shrugged. "Oh, just so that I can have a little forceful persuasion up my sleeve if I fail to get what I want by ordinary negotiation. You see, these airplanes are made to my own design, and though not as invulnerable as my *Ultra* they are definitely far ahead of the ancient fighter aircraft possessed by this country. Since the end of the United Nations war the concentration has been on civil aircraft instead of military, so with the weapons I have installed in these fifty machines, and with fifty courageous and fully trained girls to fly them, I have nothing to fear."

Bee turned from the window slowly and sank down in a chair.

"Only now do I begin to gauge the real height and depth of your plans, Vi. You mean to destroy the country, don't you? Twist men and women to do your bidding?"

"Twist is not exactly the right word, Bee. I have far reaching ideals. I believe the people of this country will conform to the policy I have in mind because by now they are desperate enough to accept anything."

"You speak as though it is a simple thing to carry your policy to the country ... You are going to need an awful lot of leaflets."

Vi smiled and motioned to her desk. She seated herself at it and Bee drew' up a chair and settled to face her.

"A little over a year ago, Bee, I made you an offer. I asked you to work side by side with me — and you refused. That being so you cannot expect any privileges here. You will simply fit yourself to whatever work I decide for you once my regime is established ... It is pretty clear that you do not appreciate how much power I really have. Here for instance you only see a part of my resources. In other parts of the country, all connected with this desk, I have my printing department — where my leaflets are prepared; my own radio station, where I have hetrodyners capable of damping out all ordinary radio bands while my own wavelength holds the air … Yes, believe me, I have made every plan to get this country under my control, and the law will never find me, particularly when those who might give me away — you for instance — are under my direct attention. You will have every comfort here, Bee, but you will not be allowed any contact with the outer world until I am ready for it —"

"You can't do this to me!" Bee cried, jumping up. "For one thing I have to keep in touch with Mother and be sure how she is progressing. There are still laws in the land and I can enforce them. You can't keep me here against my will!"

"Start realising the truth, Bee!" Vi snapped, also rising. "Down here *I* am the law, and none of the ordinary law operates. You will do exactly as I order for as long as I decide. Let that be clearly understood — once and for all."

She pressed a button and an emotionless woman of middle age came in and waited.

"Miss Munroe," Vi said, "this is my foster sister, Beatrice Brant. She will be staying with us indefinitely. Please show her to her room, give her every attention, but see to it that she has no contact with the outer world."

"Very well." The woman looked at Bee dispassionately and jerked her head. "This way, please."

Bee hesitated, gave Vi one long look of contempt, then turned and followed the woman from the office …

For a moment or two Vi sat thinking, then before her mental vision there rose Joseph Millbank, and a memory of every word he had uttered. She closed her fist slowly on the desk …

CHAPTER XII

For some reason Joseph Millbank could not sleep. He lay in bed looking at the long oblong of moonlight cast through the unshaded window … After a while of lying thus — fifteen minutes perhaps — he saw the moonlight dim before a shadow, the outline of a head and slender shoulders. He lay rigid, listening, heard the window catch slide back gently. Through his eyelashes he watched a slim figure jump softly down into the moonlit area and stand watching him.

Stealthily Millbank's hand crept under his pillow and closed on the revolver which always lay there. Then in one movement he whipped the gun up and fired. The figure seemed to jolt for a moment, then it came through the smoke of the discharge and stood glaring down in unholy calm.

"The Golden Amazon!" Millbank gulped. "But — but I shot a bullet into you —"

"Bullets don't worry me, Millbank," the girl's voice broke in mercilessly. "It is only you who worries me — and I'm going to end that now! You'll never speak against me again!"

The girl's hand shot out abruptly and whipped the gun from Millbank's grasp, sent it spinning across the room. This done, she wrenched free the telephone wire from the wall and phone and swung it gently between her hands. Millbank lay watching, his eyes popping.

"I believe you favour strangulation, do you not?" the girl asked softly. "You can now try it for yourself — !"

Her hands shot forward suddenly and whipped the telephone cord round the industrialist's neck. It tightened with irresistible force.

"Now you know how I was intended to feel when you sent that roughneck to kill me," the girl murmured. "Now you know what it means to speak too freely about me to the world. This cord is going to get tighter — and tighter — Like this!"

She left the cord knotted and watched the final thrashings of the gross form amidst the bedclothes. It was not a pretty picture … Then she turned to the window again, sidled out into the moonlit night once more.

The newspaper headlines and the radio were carrying the murder of Joseph Millbank very prominently the following morning. To Vi, who had returned to her headquarters in the night and spent an hour dislodging the magnate's bullet from her arm, there was something definitely amusing in reading of the difficulties of the police in trying to discover who had committed the crime. It was obvious, however, that one man knew who was responsible, and he wasted no time in getting in touch.

Towards mid-morning the bell of the private telephone wire buzzed sharply in Vi's office.

"Yes?" she said quietly, into the transmitter.

"Miss Brant? Are you prepared to talk with Abner Mainwaring over the phone?" It was the voice of her chief woman agent, level and composed. "He has telephoned our salon here and insists on speaking to you personally."

"Very well. Connect him through …"

There was a pause, then Mainwaring's voice came through, surprisingly eager.

"Miss Brant? I felt I would like to have a word with you —"

"What have I in common with you that you should wish for that?"

"We can soon have very much in common, believe me!"

"I suppose," the girl said dryly, "the mysterious death of Joseph Millbank hasn't prompted you to this?"

"No — no, I assure you. The truth is that I have imagination enough to realise that in the long run your ambitions are more than likely to meet with success, and out of that a new business order is bound to arise. For that reason I want to see if we cannot come to some sort of arrangement before real change is upon us. After all, the first law of business is anticipation."

Vi sat in silence, thinking.

"Did you hear me?" Mainwaring asked anxiously, after a while.

"Yes, I heard you. I was just considering. It is rather a difficult operation for me to visit you, yet it is probably more convenient to my plans than for you to visit me. Yes, I'll come and see what propositions you have to offer. You can expect me at your home about ten o'clock this evening — and a word of warning. If this is a trap you will be the one to suffer, not me.

"It is not a trap, I promise you!" Mainwaring declared.

"Very well, then. Ten tonight. Good-bye ..."

*

It was quite dark when the girl's *Ultra* landed in the park at Mainwaring's home. The moment she made herself known she was conducted to the library where Mainwaring was obviously waiting for her.

"This is an honour, Miss Brant!" he remarked, shaking hands. "Please be seated, won't you?"

He drew forth a chair for her, studying her unusual beauty.

It was the first time he had seen her face to face.

"We have nothing to gain by exchanging flatteries, Mr. Mainwaring," she remarked brusquely. "What is it you wish to see me about?"

He seated himself opposite her.

"Well, as I said, I think we can do a lot for each other. For the sake of my future safety I am willing to place all my resources at your disposal ... You see, I would much rather be your friend than your enemy."

"What resources have you?" the girl asked bluntly. "Up to now you have always worked in secret."

"I have — atomic force," Mainwaring said, calmly.

"You are sure?" The girl's intense eyes studied his jovial looking face with its innocent smile. "There are many forms of energy which scientists have mistaken for atomic force. To have discovered it means that you have unlocked the basic energy of the universe."

"I know. That I am prepared to hand it over to you is a guarantee of my good faith, isn't it?"

Vi relaxed in her chair and fingered her chin thoughtfully. "Atomic force," she said at length, "is something which I quite understand, of course, though not in the way you mean it. I have mastered it far enough to produce gold from base metals. Transmutation of elements. But it is a difficult process, and, of itself, of little commercial value."

Mainwaring leaned forward urgently. "I am referring to *real* atomic force from uranium. Over twenty years ago, in 1939 to be exact, a party of scientists from various countries stumbled on atomic force. The newspapers carried the details. For instance, the *Sunday Express* for

April 30th of that year gave the discovery front page headlines. At that time scientists were on the verge of discovering how to treat uranium in order to extract its energy: in other words, how to make a pound of uranium produce the energy of twenty million tons of coal! They were working on the new neutron process of disintegration, a vastly improved version of Lord Rutherford's first efforts to smash the atom with protons in the year 1919 …"

The girl waited, listening. Mainwaring continued with the same earnestness.

"The trouble in 1939, however, was that the scientists feared the effect of their work might be progressive — that smashing one atom of uranium with protons would cause the atom to give off more neutrons and the thing would go on and on, even to the point of bringing about the destruction of the earth itself." Mainwaring paused, and reflected. "Well, then came war and we heard no more of these experiments. I was a comparatively young man, then, interested in this new discovery but unable to keep track of it because of the sudden censorship imposed by war. The moment the war was over, though, I investigated. I followed out the experiments of these scientists for myself, and at last after a lot of failures I produced true atomic force. And it is fully controllable. I have a private laboratory hidden away from the world where my engineers have been at work for a long time making bombs — vastly explosive bombs, one of which could obliterate the centre of London alone."

A strange look came to the girl's face.

"Bombs! But for why?"

"Well, before Millbank — er — died we had ideas on the overthrow of this lazy Government of ours, but that is out of court now. There are of course better, or at least more domesticated, uses for atomic force than to make it into bombs. For instance, atomic force can be used for the lighting of cities, the fuelling of engines, the driving of ships … And so on."

Again Mainwaring found the girl's piercing eyes fixed on him.

"And you made this discovery?" she asked.

"I did."

"And for the sake of compromise and the assurance of safety when I take control you are prepared to hand over the discovery to me for purely peaceful uses?"

"That is my offer — and it is worth it to me in order to assure my future. I think I am right in assuming that with all your scientific skill you do not possess atomic force in this form."

"Quite right," the girl admitted. "It has persistently eluded me up till now. To happen on the right combination, to unleash such a terrifying power, is not so much a matter of mathematical calculation as of luck. You had the luck. And with a secret like, that I could transform the world!"

"I hope," Mainwaring murmured, "we can do business."

"And if I should refuse your offer?" the girl asked after a while.

Mainwaring still smiled like a cherub.

"I do not think you would be so short sighted. You have admitted that atomic force is the one thing you have not got, and you are scientist enough to know that against it your own scientific appliances could not stand for long. If you do not bargain with me and take the secret in return for guaranteeing my immunity in the new order then I shall go to work against you, reveal that you murdered Joseph Millbank — for you certainly did — and arrange it that your secret hideout is discovered and destroyed with atomic bombs. I could do it, you know. I am not without agents any more than you are ..."

"Strange," the girl mused, "you haven't attempted something of the sort already instead of bargaining with me."

"I like to be kind to people," Mainwaring smiled. "And as I have said, I prefer an assured future to risking my life."

"I see — and I think I should remind you that if I decide to reject your offer I shall act so swiftly that you will never have the time to find my hideout, as you fondly imagine."

"I'll risk it ..." Mainwaring lighted a cigar and lay back in his chair, watching the girl through the blue haze.

She got to her feet and paced about for a while. Then she came back and asked a blunt question.

"Just how do I know that all this is true?"

"I can give you any proof you want."

"Very well, then; if you can show me what an atomic force bomb can do, I think we can compromise. Not otherwise. I only deal in facts."

"And wisely." Mainwaring thought for a moment, then asked a question. "You have your own plane here, of course?"

The girl looked surprised. "Well, yes ..."

"Good! If you are prepared to make a short journey, I think I can satisfy you completely. But we shall have to use your machine; mine is being overhauled."

A vague suspicion touched Vi's mind. She tried hard to judge the workings of that inscrutable brain, but without success.

"How far is the journey?" she asked abruptly.

"Not more than twenty minutes flying time."

She nodded and turned to the door. Mainwaring accompanied her into the hall, got into his hat and coat, then followed her outside. In a few minutes they were in the *Ultra's* cabin and the girl was at the controls. Smoothly they were borne into the air. For some time there was silence between them. Then —

"Strange, isn't it," Mainwaring said, "that we two — enemies — should be up here together?"

"Not when we have a common purpose," the girl replied.

He glanced at her face in the dashboard light and beheld it grimly set. Then he relaxed in his seat again, gazing through the window at the stars, listening to the sighing of the night wind against the thick hull. Now and again he gave brief directions as to the course to be taken, finally pointing below.

"That's where we're heading. See anything?"

The girl looked through the window but failed to distinguish anything beyond the countryside in the uncertain moonlight.

"Go lower," Mainwaring said, then as she did so he gave a sardonic chuckle. "Good camouflage, eh?"

She saw what he meant now. Not until the *Ultra* was directly over the point of landing did she see that what she had taken for a meadow was actually an immense, cleverly disguised roof. The camouflage was not far short of the perfection she had achieved for her own hidden domain.

Finally, under Mainwaring's directions, she brought the *Ultra* to the ground within a few yards of the concealed spot. Mainwaring led the way outside, pausing at a trapdoor let into the ground.

"Follow me," he said, and raising the trapdoor he flashed a torch beam down a flight of steps. In silence the girl followed him, keeping her hand on the gun in her pocket for instant use.

Then Mainwaring opened a door and strode into an underground expanse of brilliant light and activity. Vi looked about her, frankly astonished. The place was strikingly similar to her own retreat. Everywhere she looked there were machines — monstrous electrical devices. She recognized vacuum tubes, bar-magnets, great banks of insulators, all the complicated impedimenta demanded by a research physicist. And dominating the whole vast array were two monstrous globes perched on slender pillars, between which there roared and flashed a titanic voltage of electricity — man made chain lightning. For a time Vi watched it, fascinated, could feel the static in the air setting the roots of her hair tingling.

"You are watching the manufacture of atomic bombs," Mainwaring shouted over the din. "In case it doesn't satisfy you take a look at this …"

He turned to where a man in a lead protective uniform was working at a machine and said something to him. The man nodded and handed over an object the size of a walnut. Holding it tightly between finger and thumb Mainwaring returned to the girl's side.

"Small size atomic force bomb," he explained. "Filled with uranium filings and with a detonator supplying an electric charge. In other words, enough force in this tiny object to blow a small sized city to pieces."

"I would still prefer you to prove it," the girl answered.

"Then I shall. Come with me."

He picked up an instrument rather like an old-fashioned musket and then led the way out to the surface again. In the moonlight the girl could see him fitting the bomb into the firing chamber of the "musket."

"This gun is used for testing," he explained. "When I press the button the bomb will be hurled three miles distant. Just the same we shall have to throw ourselves flat because of the blast. Now, are you ready?"

She nodded, and a moment later the switch clicked. They both lay down on their faces and waited — Then all of a sudden the dark silence of the night sky was split by a monstrous glare of white fanning upwards against the horizon. A few seconds later came the sound — the rolling reverberation of a tremendous explosion. The ground rocked as though with earthquake and despite the distance the stupendous blast hurled pieces of debris into the air, deluging the two in dust as they waited for the disturbance to pass.

"I hope," Mainwaring remarked, getting to his feet at length, "that you are now quite satisfied? You can imagine what a full sized bomb would do when one the size of a walnut can do that!"

The girl nodded slowly. "All right, Mainwaring, I'm quite satisfied —"

"I am too," he interrupted suddenly, and before she had the chance to anticipate him he had pulled a high-powered automatic from his pocket and levelled it at her.

"What's the idea, Mainwaring?"

"Don't tell me you haven't guessed," he answered bitterly. "I've taken a tremendous gamble to get you alone — to destroy you without implicating myself. I dare not kill you after the things you did to Sidcombe's man, to Sidcombe himself, to Meller, and then to Millbank. I had to think of something sufficiently unusual to tempt you out of your lair, so I gambled with my secret of atomic force —"

"In plain language you mean to kill me?"

"Naturally. I have no intention of trading secrets with you; I am only interested in getting rid of you before you become too strong for me. The way I have worked things out I can be rid of you all right, and without incriminating myself."

"I see," the girl said, her voice deadly quiet. "I don't quite see why, knowing you intended doing this, you took the trouble to demonstrate an atomic bomb."

"It was essential you should know about it. From what I have heard your physique can withstand bullets, and besides, were you found, even dead, the bullets could be traced back to me. But if on the other hand you are blown to fragments by an atomic bomb — ! Well, there just won't be any traces. That is why I showed you the power of these bombs. Securely bound in your own *Ultra* with a delayed action bomb in the cabin with you, you can imagine the result. If pieces of your ship are found it will simply be assumed that it blew to atoms in mid-air through some defect or other."

"I wouldn't be too sure of myself if I were you, Mainwaring," Vi said slowly.

"Why not? I know a bullet can disable you even if it doesn't kill you, and in that time I can carry you into your ship and —"

Suddenly, with bewildering speed, the girl leapt at him. He could not fire his gun so he struck out with it savagely. By a sheer fluke his blow was a lucky one for it caught the girl a violent blow on the temple and knocked her sprawling on the ground.

For a moment Mainwaring was puzzled at the ease of his victory. He went forward cautiously, suspecting a trick, but when he turned the girl face upward he realised that she was completely unconscious. Smiling to himself he lifted her in his arms and carried her to the *Ultra*, dumped her in the driving seat and then proceeded to fasten her with strong wire from the emergency kit. He bound her ankles and wrists three times. He felt convinced in the end that there was no way in which she could escape.

The task finished, he hurried back to the underground factory and returned in a few minutes with a bomb about the size of an orange. Adjusting the mechanism, he placed it under the driving seat. To put in the delayed action automatic pilot on the switchboard was only the work of a moment, and he fixed it so that the *Ultra* would cruise in a wide circle at a five mile altitude ... Then he climbed outside and slammed the cabin door.

From a distance he watched the machine take off a few minutes later in a clean, level sweep and then begin to climb swiftly into the sky. He smiled as he watched it go ...

*

Vi returned to her senses slowly, trying to recall exactly what had happened to her. She tried to raise a hand to her aching head and the discovery that she was pinned to her seat brought back remembrance in a sudden rush.

Immediately she grasped the situation, became aware of her slowly circling vessel and the subdued ticking of something not very far away. She recalled Mainwaring's threat too and cursed the lucky blow that had given him the advantage. Vaguely she wondered why he had not killed her and placed her corpse in the machine to be blown to pieces — unless the fear that some part of her body with the tell-tale bullet in it had made him hold his hand

Anyway this was no time for speculation. She began straining her wrists and ankles to the utmost, winced at the pain from the wire as it bit into hr flesh. After a while she desisted and looked about her, listened to the ticking of the thing under the seat. There was no way of telling how long it would be before it blew her to eternity. If only there were some way to be rid of it — rolling it to the floor trap somehow and so disposing of it …

Suddenly her eyes lighted on something — the wire-clippers in the tool rack. But it was too far away. Perhaps, though … She strained herself forward with every ounce of her immense strength, until abruptly the bolts holding the seat in the floor parted company with the nuts and sent her tumbling forward. She struck her chin a violent blow on the control board and relaxed for a moment until the pain subsided. Then she strained forward desperately, inching her head forward until her teeth were nearly on the clippers … A bit further, and she felt their coldness between her lips. Savagely she pulled at them and they fell free to the bench below the control board. Again she picked them up in her teeth and dropped them to her lap, jerking her left leg up as far as she could to tilt them sideways. At last they reached the edge of her leg and she made the final effort — and missed. She could not bring her bound hands far enough from behind her back to seize them and they clinked to the floor.

She breathed hard and tossed the hair out of her eyes, then leaning backwards she forced the loosened, rocking seat to fall over with a bang, causing her to strike her head on the floor violently. She looked sideways and saw that devilish, ticking bomb not three inches from her face … But there was something else. Her wrists were pressing, painfully indeed, into the hard outlines of the clippers. Scraping and scratching with her fingers, she got them in her grip at last and snipped through the wire holding her wrists together.

The rest was easy. In a moment her ankles were free. She dived immediately for the bomb and hurled it through the floor trap into space. Before it could have been anywhere near the ground it exploded. The sky was as livid as daylight for a few moments and the recoiling blast sent the *Ultra* sweeping upwards helplessly, to come back on level keel when the disturbance had subsided.

Vi scrambled over to the controls, swung the vessel round, then drove from the heights to the lower levels of the air. Her blue eyes had the light of murder in them as she stared fixedly through the observation window — and at last she caught sight of that skilful camouflage protecting Mainwaring's domain. Immediately she came down to ground level and brought her machine to a halt. Hurrying over to the door she jumped to the ground outside. Day was just beginning to dawn ...

Her movement towards the concealed entrance to the factory was interrupted, however, as she caught sight of a one-seater plane coming up from a concealed ramp leading from underground. Instantly she tugged out her flame pistol and fired.

The needle of incandescence struck the engine and burst it into flames. The cabin door flew open and Mainwaring appeared precipitately, gazing round as though to discover the cause of the mishap. Immediately his eyes fell on the *Ultra*. He suddenly comprehended the situation as he caught sight of the girl advancing slowly towards him with gun in hand.

"You!" he breathed. "You set fire to my plane!"

"Get into that factory of yours," the girl ordered in a level voice.

"Now wait a minute!" he protested. "Just because you have somehow escaped —"

The girl's icy voice cut him short. "Either do as you are told, Mainwaring, or I'll drop you where you stand. I won't kill you because I want information, but I'll slice off your ears with this flame gun of mine for a start. Do you want that? Now — *get into that factory*!"

Sullen faced, he obeyed, opened the trap and went down the steps. The gun remained fixed in his neck while the girl came down behind him, then when they reached the level floor it, descended to the small of his back. But when he got to the inner door of the factory itself he struck out savagely. The sudden blow knocked the girl's gun from her grasp, but her left fist came up with unbelievable speed and back of it was all the force of her supernormal muscles. Mainwaring lifted right off his feet, crashed into the half open door, then went sprawling against the nearest machine ...

The various workers stared, then the girl recovered her gun and came quietly in.

"Don't try any tricks with me, Mainwaring," she advised. "When I was prepared to compromise with you, you double crossed me and did your best to kill me. I'm not going to forget that. I'm glad, however, that your eagerness to develop your plan forced you into showing me this factory. I'm giving you an ultimatum here and now. Either hand to me the secret of atomic force within ten minutes, or this factory and all it contains, you included, will be blown sky high by a squadron of my own airplanes, for which I have radioed." Mainwaring got to his feet slowly, gave an ugly laugh. "Do you expect me to believe that?"

"Yes, because unless I get that secret I shall not leave here, and the fact that I *don't* leave will be the signal for the destruction of this place to commence."

Mainwaring bit his lower lip savagely and gazed round on the workers. There were about six of them, most of them attired in their lead-protective suits and hoods.

"Better do it, chief —" one of them started to say, but Mainwaring silenced him with an angry gesture. Then he looked back at the girl.

"Your bluff doesn't work, Miss Brant. You won't have this building blown up as long as you are in it. And I don't believe you have any planes either!"

She smiled coldly. "You have seven and a half minutes left. I've taken the risk of death to achieve my object. I'm not afraid of it even if you are."

Her words started a decided flurry of anxiety amongst the workers. They glanced at each other through their face glasses and then glanced anxiously at the big clock slicing off the seconds. Suddenly they started as a shaft of flame blazed past Mainwaring's right ear. He fell back, rubbing the ugly burn which had been blistered right across his cheek.

"Remember me remarking about your ears?" the girl asked, smiling only with her lips. "I don't like waiting!"

"You can go on waiting, damn you!" he screamed. "You —"

"He can't give you the secret," one of the employees blurted out from behind his helmet. "It isn't his to give!"

Vi glanced at the worker sharply. Smaller in stature than the others, with a high falsetto voice, he was pushing his way to the front, fingering the clasps about his neck to unfasten the helmet.

"You shut up!" Mainwaring roared at him. "This is no affair of yours —"

"I think it is," the girl snapped. "Let him speak."

Mainwaring glanced about him desperately, suddenly made a dive to stop the worker removing his helmet — but the lashing fire of the girl's gun seared suddenly across his other ear and sent him reefing back with a scream of pain. In those split seconds his ear had been charred black.

"I said — let him speak!" Vi repeated — then she gave an astonished look, for it was not a man who had emerged from behind the protective lead coverings but a woman — forty-five perhaps, though her greying hair made her look older. The face was lined and resignedly calm. Only in the clear blue eyes did there still sparkle a light of quick intelligence.

"A — woman!" Vi whispered. "You discovered atomic force?"

"And have been a captive ever since," she assented quietly. "This is the first time I have had the chance to make an escape. I have been imprisoned here, forced to work for this ambitious, grasping devil."

"But you know the secret of atomic force?" Vi insisted, seizing her arm.

"Certainly I do. Without me nothing can be done. That is why I am here ..."

"You damnable, dirty —" Mainwaring could find no more words to say. The anguish of his ear was too much for him; this and the betrayal of his secret hopes. Unable to control himself he lunged forward in blind rage ...

Vi did not stop him: instead she sidestepped neatly, still holding the woman by the arm, whirled her to the doorway. In a moment they were both through it. Vi slammed the door shut and then turned her flame gun on the lock. Instantly it fused into a mass of metal, effectually blocking any attempt that might be made to operate it.

"You're — you're trapping them!" the woman exclaimed.

"You've no regard for them, have you?"

"Well, no —"

"That's all that matters then. Come on — quick."

Vi forced the woman quickly up the short tunnel to the exterior steps. As they ascended they heard the hammering of fists on the jammed door, impassioned cries for release — Then, outside, the sounds died away. The woman looked overhead.

"I don't see any planes ..."

"Pure bluff," Vi shrugged. "But I have them just the same, ready when needed."

With that she piloted the bewildered woman through the grey dawn light to the *Ultra*. They settled themselves. Then when they had risen perhaps two hundred feet Vi bent the ship's nose down, levelled her twin guns and fired them right at the camouflaged area below.

The explosion which followed was incredible in its violence. The upward and outward blast hurled the *Ultra* through the air with dizzying speed, demanding every ounce of Vi's skill to get it on to even keel again. Gradually she managed it, then sat with her hands on the switches staring back through the rear port at a titanic smoking crater gouged in the earth.

The woman she had rescued turned a pale, strained face.

"Those atomic bombs which were stored there must have exploded. Thank heaven they were only small ones and none too many of them, otherwise … Just what did you use in those guns?"

"Disintegrator beams. They blasted right through the roof. I have a fancy," Vi reflected, "that Abner Mainwaring will not trouble society again."

"Or those other employees — all of them innocent."

"The innocent suffering for the guilty," Vi shrugged.

The woman was silent for a moment, then she said quietly:

"You are the Golden Amazon, aren't you?" Then as Vi nodded, "It seems that all I have heard about you is more or less true."

"You mean the radio report?" Vi asked.

"That is the only way since I have been in captivity. Radio was not barred to us. I have followed your activities with a good deal of interest, but the one thing I did not expect was that you would walk into the enemy camp and rescue me."

"Was there no way of defeating Mainwaring? No way of escape?"

"Neither for me or those men. The laboratory-factory which you saw had an extension beyond — a kind of underground home for us. We had every comfort, good meals, everything we could wish for except liberty. The radio was the only way of keeping in touch with events in the outside world. As I have told you, it is over a year since I have seen the daylight."

The woman stopped talking and looked through the window toward the rising sun. A faint smile of pleasure hovered round her colourless mouth.

"Did Mainwaring kidnap you?" Vi asked presently.

"I suppose that is really what he did. He tricked me quite legally into working for him and arranged a contract whereby my disappearance seemed quite logical to the world … You see, ever since the end of the war I have been interested in science. During that war I lost both my husband and my daughter in air raids. To save myself from brooding over the loss and also to try and get some money together when the war was over, I took up physical research, in which I had always been interested. I followed out the idea of the scientists who had been working on uranium, and more by luck than judgment stumbled on genuine atomic force. Providence must have been on my side in that I didn't blow myself to pieces but released the energy gradually.

"Rather foolishly, for I had made plenty of money with other scientific gadgets, I approached Mainwaring with the idea of using the discovery to benefit the world. Knowing him to be an industrialist with a good deal of influence I didn't see that I was making a mistake until it was too late. He simply used me, knowing I must be a first-class scientist by very reason of the fact that I was rewarded with the Diploma of Merit some years ago for my work ... My name incidentally is Irene Grayson."

"Obviously," Vi said, "you never advertised your discovery to the world, otherwise I'd have known it."

"I was afraid for what might happen. Later I regretted it because I realised that if the public had only known something they might have looked into my disappearance."

Vi gave her a reassuring smile. "Well, Irene, your captivity is all over now. You shall be elevated to the heights worthy of your scientific ability. In my regime — and it is bound to come — you will be a leading scientist. Between us — you with your knowledge and I with mine — what can we not do to improve this muddled world?"

"You can be sure of my support," Irene Grayson said, her tired eyes searching the girl's face. "I admire your endeavours, the stand you are making for women generally. This lazy Government we have definitely needs shaking up."

"I fancy it will get it —"

Vi broke off and glanced below.

"This is where we land ... My secret headquarters."

CHAPTER XIII

As Vi and Irene Grayson entered the private office they found Beatrice there, her face white and haggard. She came forward immediately as the two entered.

"This is my foster sister, Beatrice Brant," Vi said, with a wave of her hand. "Bee, meet Irene Grayson, the woman who has discovered —"

"I've just had the most dreadful news," Bee interrupted, too worried to give any greeting to the woman. "A message has come through from home that Mother is … is dead. She passed away in the early hours of this morning."

Vi was silent for a moment, then she compressed her lips. "That is bad news — for you, Bee —"

"You've got to let me go and see her! You've *got* to!"

"I'm sorry." Vi shook her head adamantly. "Nobody who has ever been here is allowed to leave, and you are no exception. I will make arrangements for Mother to be buried with Father tomorrow — a double funeral."

Bee stared through eyes that were brimming with tears. "Vi, I must go! I beg of you … You can't be so cruel as to stop me —"

"Get back to your room, Bee, and stop behaving like a child!" Vi ordered harshly. "Go on — out! We have business to discuss here, Irene and I."

Bee half hesitated, her face colouring with vindictive fury — then without another word she turned and went.

"At least you are not over sentimental," Irene Grayson remarked, seating herself. "The poor girl's feelings are quite understandable, you know."

"Her feelings are less important than my safety, Irene, and that is all that matters. And I think you should know from now on that the same rule about nobody leaving here applies to you as well."

The woman smiled. "I have no wish to go, I assure you. In return for a little peace and quiet, I am quite prepared to fall in with your plans. Knowing you, I presume they'll be big ones."

Vi sat down at her desk and leaned forward earnestly. "How right you are! The time has come now to launch my radio and leaflet campaign, demanding that I be nominated as a candidate for control of the country, versus the Government. If I am nominated I know that I shall have a walk-over with the electorate and will become the first dictatress of Britain."

"And if you are *not* nominated?" Irene Grayson asked quietly.

"I shall overthrow the Government! That is an eventuality for which I am fully prepared. Now Mainwaring has transferred you into my hands I am convinced of victory. You see, you fit very definitely into the pattern."

"Of course you mean atomic force?"

"Just that. I can promise the people all the advantages that that power can bring — that is if you are prepared to hand over the formula to me."

"I will — when you achieve success. You can make the promises, all right, and I'll see they're implemented when you are elected."

Vi's expression changed.

"Listen to me, Irene. I saved your life because I expected a return — and that return is atomic force. You have nothing to gain by refusing. You can never leave here. I can give you a very high position in my new regime, all providing that you hand that secret to me."

Irene Grayson lapsed into thought for a moment or two, then at — last she said:

"I am prepared to let you have the formula on one condition — that you do not do as Mainwaring did and try and use it for destructive purposes."

"You know that my whole aim is to benefit humanity," Vi said, spreading her hands. "You have my solemn promise."

"Very well. If you will let me see your electrical laboratory I will show you the process."

"Right away." Vi got to, her feet immediately. "Then we will plan this campaign together — two expert scientists. Come along this way ..."

*

Two days later, in the early afternoon, Bee found herself with a visitor in the rooms she had been assigned. It was Irene Grayson, smiling sympathetically.

"I thought I would like a word or two with you," she explained, as Bee looked at her curiously. "That is, if you don't mind …"

"I shan't make very good company, I'm afraid," the girl sighed. "I've just had very bad news over the radio."

"I know," Irene Grayson said quietly, taking the chair Bee had drawn forward for her. "Your mother and father have been given a double funeral, your sister appointing mourners by proxy. That was why I wanted to talk to you, to console you if I can. You heard as well, I suppose, that that pilot friend of yours you've mentioned has been released following that exposé by Millbank the other day."

"Yes, I heard," Bee muttered. "I also heard that item about the police wondering where Mainwaring has gone and what caused a crater two miles wide near Lower Mordham village. Vi did that, and you would think the police would know it too … Oh, what's the use of anything, Irene? The police out searching for Vi — the Golden Amazon — and Chris helping them. And we can't do a thing to give any information … You know, it beats me why you decided to throw in your lot with her. She aims at nothing less than the domination of the country."

"I know — but I don't think that would be such a bad thing. Your sister has some most amazing ideas —"

"Please remember that she is my *foster* sister. I would much prefer not having her name coupled with mine."

"I'm sorry," Irene said quietly. "I'd forgotten you are not really related. Just how *did* you come together?"

"She is simply a survivor of the air blitz on England twenty years or so ago, whom Dad found near our home in Little Beading when I was a child. He found her in the arms of a Dr. Prout who died before he could tell anything else but her name, which was Violet Ray. Not that I can imagine you being interested …"

"Oh, but I am! This girl has such extraordinary qualities that her history makes me wonder …" Irene reflected for a moment, then she got up and patted Bee gently on the shoulder. "I shall have to be going. Vi is deep in plans and will be wondering where I am if I don't help her. She has gone to the Laboratory for an hour so I thought I'd have a word of sympathy for you because of the radio news … Be sure of one thing, Bee, I am your friend … Good-bye for now."

She went out quietly and closed the door. Bee shook her dark head moodily, then turned back to the window which gave a view on to the throbbing industry of the underworld.

*

In the days that followed Vi worked with an unprecedented vigour, contacting all her many agents, giving them special orders, and so gradually fomenting such a state of confusion among the masses of the depressed people that riots were reported from many places. Once this happened she had leaflets scattered by the thousand to the populace, in which she outlined her future policy more clearly than ever and demanded that the Government state publicly that it would hold a general election and nominate her as a candidate.

The accusations against her — the destruction of the air liner for instance — she called malicious lying, a disgraceful effort to blacken her in the eyes of the people. And because the people were about ready to listen to anything they believed her. Their argument, and a logical one, was that they could hardly be any the worse off anyway.

But the Government took no notice at all. It still did not believe that there was anybody really dangerous to contend with. A criminal, yes, whom the harassed and baffled police would soon apprehend, but as for challenging the sacrosanct power of the Government ... ! Ridiculous!

So the people grumbled and fought among themselves. To them it seemed — just as Vi had planned — that they were being refused a new deal because of the lethargy or jealousy of the Government. There were demonstrations and placards in Whitehall, mounted police and angry clashes ...

Then in the midst of the turmoil the girl played her trump card and used the radio devices she had in her underground retreat. To the country she broadcast a speech, and it was revealing in many ways in that she permitted a glimpse of the secret organization she had built up behind the scenes ... She told for the first time of the death of Mainwaring among the atomic bombs he had — so she said — been preparing to hurl down on defenceless cities. She told of the passing of the secret of atomic force to herself, then basing her confidence on the fact that she had averted terrible war she called again for the backing of the people, especially women, throughout the land. She spoke of the thousands of Leagues which had been co-ordinated by her agents under one command, and of the strategic sites which had been bought close to large cities. For the Leagues she promised complete headquarters with radio equipment before too long a time …

"So," she concluded, "the Government would do well to convene a Nomination meeting right away. I *demand* a vote! It is customary for a potential nominee to place a speaker in Parliament who will answer all questions the Government may wish to ask. For this purpose I am appointing one Irene Grayson, who will answer without bias every question put to her about me. Here then is my ultimatum: I demand that the Government give me the chance to be nominated for election, and if that comes about the public shall be permitted to vote freely as to whom they prefer for their governing body — a woman who has smashed a possible onslaught by ambitious industrialists and who can restore prosperity, or a collection of men who spend their time on holiday while want and depression are all around them." Vi closed the microphone — then looking up she found the eyes of Beatrice fixed upon her.

"You know of course that the Government will do all in its power to stop you being nominated as a candidate, don't you?"

"Naturally," the girl shrugged, "but I know too that the Government can't refuse to nominate me with so many women now on my side. I have become their champion, their leader. Also I know that you, Irene, will answer all questions with unswerving truthfulness. I cannot think of a better personal representative to state my case."

"By what right can you enter Parliament?" Bee asked, looking at her.

"Right of Merit," Irene replied calmly. "It is the rule of the present Constitution that a man or woman possessing a Diploma of Merit is permitted to enter Parliament and attend any debate. I can exercise that right — and I shall. I received the Diploma of Merit for my researches into atomic force. It confers the freedom of the city, and to a great extent replaces the one time Nobel Prize."

Bee shrugged and turned away, left the office. Vi looked at the closed door, then turned back to Irene Grayson.

"Listen, Irene, this means everything to me. I've got to get nomination; I've got to!"

"You can rely on me to do what I can, you know that …"

CHAPTER XIV

Alarmed at the crisis precipitated by the Golden Amazon and urged by public demand through press and radio, the Prime Minister, Sir Robert Haslam, finally decided to convene a Nomination Meeting in the House for four o'clock in the afternoon following the girl's broadcast.

Sir Robert, a gaunt-faced man with iron grey hair, seemed fully aware of the gravity of the situation as he rose to his feet after the Speaker's preliminary address. Looking round on the faces it filled him with some uneasiness when he noted at least half a dozen women who had risen to commercial eminence since the end of the United Nations War. They could make telling trouble for him — and probably would.

Then he commenced talking, slowly, and for a long time it was obvious that he was merely recounting what everybody knew. He traced the Amazon's lightning rise to a position of dangerous power, and so finally reached the reason for the meeting — Should this Golden Amazon be nominated for election or not? This began a storm of argument.

Calver Grant, free speaker for the Government, was dead against the idea — but Cynthia Drew, woman industrialist, was firmly in agreement with the Amazon's intended policy. Then Irene Grayson, as the girl's representative, was called upon to state her views. She gave them with perfect honesty and made it clear that the Amazon's scientific prowess was of a quality to reckon with. If she failed to get nomination it was possible she might do many things — dangerous things.

"And if she *does* get nominated, and then elected," Calver Grant said, "she'll drive men right out of office. She hates men as a sex; I'm convinced of it. The mastery of Britain by this woman, I believe, is only the beginning. It is but a short step after that to the other countries — the whole world. I say gather together everything we've got and thrash her."

"Absurd!" Cynthia Drew said coldly. "I am entirely in support of her nomination."

"Naturally," the Government representative sneered. "You are a woman, and in a woman's rule you foresee a vast influx of prosperity for your various businesses which are now in a deplorable condition."

"I know men couldn't make it any better," Cynthia Drew retorted.

There was a long, bitter pause — then Irene Grayson spoke again, and it was to dwell strongly on the benefits of atomic force if used in the right way, and to stress even more heavily the impossibility of beating the Amazon's scientific weapons. But the moment she sat down again the irrepressible Calver Grant jumped up again.

"Rubbish!" he shouted. "We still have weapons, the material to smash this madwoman —"

"There is another witness," the Prime Minister broke in, and looking round the assembly he gave a nod. To the surprise of most people it was Chris Wilson who stood up.

"I had Mr. Wilson summoned from his flying duties so he could make a statement about the Golden Amazon," the Prime Minister explained. "I have also given him the chance to read certain records. Proceed, Mr. Wilson."

"Fight her!" Chris cried, without hesitation. "We are not fighting an ordinary woman but a scientific freak —"

"I challenge that!" Irene Grayson interrupted hotly.

"I'll answer it!" Chris turned to her. "Before he left for Europe on the liner in which he met his death, Dr. Meller gave a statement to the police regarding the medical facts of this woman. Since I have been helping the police I have had the chance to read the statement very thoroughly —"

"*What* medical facts?" Irene Grayson asked sharply. Almost word for word Chris repeated the statement he had read, outlining completely the facts of the operation performed on the girl — or at least the facts as Meller had imagined they must have been. When he was finished Chris added:

"That there was a Dr. James Axton I have proved from the medical *Who's Who* of 1940, and also at that time Dr. Meller was head of the Institute referred to …"

"And further," the Prime Minister said, "there are two records here. One refers to a meeting of the Medical Research Institute on August 30, 1940" — he held up a sheaf of papers — "and the other is a statement from the Ministry of Home Security dated the same year. The first statement says that the Institute refused the application of a Dr. James Axton — sponsored by a Dr. Prout — to perform a gland experiment on a female child. Axton stated that he would make his experiment in face of the edict and was debarred for that reason … The other statement reports that Dr. Axton was found in the ruins of his home at Little Beading, on August 31st following a heavy and indiscriminate air raid on the district."

"I believe," Chris Wilson said, "that Axton got a child from somewhere on which to experiment and that the Golden Amazon is that child, grown to womanhood." There was a long silence, then the Prime Minister looked across at Irene Grayson questioningly.

"I have nothing further to say," she said, in a very quiet voice.

There were surprised looks cast towards her. The Prime Minister shrugged and nodded to the usher to commence handing out the voting papers. It was an hour later when the electric sorter had recorded its decision.

"This woman shall not be nominated!" the Prime Minister stated. "We shall fight her instead! The actual figures are —" But his words were drowned out by the roar of voices. Irene Grayson got to her feet and looked across to where Chris Wilson was sitting. Their eyes met for a moment … Then she turned and went out …

*

Back at the underground retreat Irene Grayson found Vi in her office with Beatrice seated opposite her. Apparently they had both been listening to the radio-televizor.

Vi's eyes were flaming as she glanced up.

"I've just had the report," she breathed. "Your confounded muteness and Wilson's evidence destroyed my chances. Why the devil couldn't you have spoken for me?"

"In the face of such evidence," Irene shrugged, "there was little I could say."

"Pathological freak, eh?" the girl muttered, clenching her fist. "That's become public knowledge now. I was told it long ago by Meller, but what does it matter? By heaven, Irene, I'll smash this doddering Government wide open for that! I'll bury their ancient ideas under the ruins of London! I'll wreck their whole blasted city! What difference does it make what my history is? I'm a flesh and blood woman, aren't I?

147

If I were a product of a test tube I could understand their hatred. As it is, it simply doesn't make sense …"

"Though I couldn't defend you very well I am still loyal to you," Irene Grayson said.

There was a brief silence, then Vi started speaking again, half to herself.

"Irene, in spite of what I promised, I am going to use atomic force for bombing purposes! I haven't found it very difficult to make atomic bombs, anyway, once I got the basic formula. In fact, I have had one of my factories do nothing else, just in case there was a contingency like this. The fifty planes I have ready will drop them in relays. The sites I have bought near various cities can be used as airfields. I will attack London first, and if that has no effect other cities will feel the anguish. I refuse to be beaten, understand? Not after all the plans I have made. Another thing I must do is broadcast to those who wish to stand by me and tell them to report at the League Headquarters nearest their particular cities and receive instructions from my agents. By the time I have made that broadcast the news will be published that the Government has refused to nominate me for election …"

The girl beat her clenched fist softly on the desk.

"Yes — that's it!" Then she turned to the private wire telephone and switched it on. In a few moments she was talking to her chief agent at the Plus Clothing Company.

" … and these are your orders," she said, when the preliminaries had been dispensed with. "You will prepare to handle whatever women arrive at League Headquarters after the broadcast I am shortly going to make. You will arm yourselves as best you can and enter the city nearest to your respective headquarters. In regard to men, particularly armed ones or pilots, give them no help and if necessary shoot them. Leave London itself out of your activities and get as many women away from the city as are loyal. I intend to bomb the city tonight. I shall issue a radio ultimatum to the Government to either reverse their decision concerning my nomination or take the consequences. The ultimatum will expire at midnight. You understand?"

"Completely," the voice replied. "I will pass the word on, Miss Brant."

The girl switched off and relapsed into thought. When she looked up again she found Beatrice and Irene Grayson had both left her to herself.

Inwardly she wondered if their actions had been intended as a measure of their contempt for her decision …

*

The Golden Amazon's ultimatum came with such suddenness that the public had hardly any time to adjust itself. Here and there were women who perceived that they would be safer at a League headquarters than in the heart of a city and so they promptly bent their steps in that direction. They were single women mainly, young, and filled with the thirst for adventure. The older ones had too many responsibilities to just desert them at a moment's notice. So gradually there began to hurry through the evening a swelling stream of women …

In Whitehall also events were moving fast. Chris Wilson found himself summoned for an audience with a hastily planned emergency committee at the head of which was the Prime Minister. In five minutes he discovered that he had been placed in command of the London airplane defence squadrons and so immediately departed for his station at the London Central Airport.

Certainly there was no sign of reversing decision in regard to the girl's nomination. While she sat waiting at her radio apparatus in her underground office, Bee and Irene her only companions and both of them making ineffectual efforts to make her hold her hand, events were moving rapidly in other directions. Radio summonses were going forth every five minutes to different army stations. Reserves were being called up. Airplanes, woefully weak in weapons, moved over to strategic airdromes, mainly near London, and so came under Chris Wilson's direct command.

He had the feeling that his ground work would not be for long; that he would be compelled to take the air before the night was out and use every trick he knew in a plane to try and defeat the attackers. He was under no illusion regarding the power of the girl's science: he had too many uncomfortably strong examples of it for that. He would have been even more worried had he known that each of her machines was equipped with television eyes and that from her own headquarters she could watch the battle with comparative omniscience, enjoying an immense advantage denied to the hastily prepared defenders.

Yes, it was going to be hard, going brutally hard, but not for a moment would Chris admit, even to himself, that there was a possibility of defeat. That was too ghastly a thought to even be entertained …

Until eleven-thirty he was kept constantly busy arranging the deployment of his squadrons by radio, then when he felt he had done all in his power he went up to the top of the control tower for a breath of fresh air. For a long time he stood at the rail gazing out over the city. It was as strange a view as any he had ever seen, so different from the accustomed picture of light and prosperity before the advent of this devil woman. It was the same kind of scene on which his father and mother must have gazed, and probably with similar misgivings.

The metropolis lay blacked out under a full moon. Hadn't his father used to call it a "bombers' moon"? Vague remembrances stirred him … Nowhere in the streets was there the mere glimmer of a light. Gone were the monstrous floodlamps which had etched out the principal edifices; gone too were the neon lines which had distinguished road from pedestrian way. London lay silent, split by the flowing silver of the Thames.

Chris smiled rather bitterly to himself — then he glanced above. The night was perfect. In these conditions and with the moon rapidly climbing, his few but stout fighters might be able to give a good account of themselves. In any event the battle would no doubt be fought out at a great height for the stratosphere was the generally accepted ceiling.

Then Big Ben began to strike midnight. Chris turned back to the lift and returned to the control room in the basement. Every other official at his post, keeping a careful watch on the illumined map of the entire country. High up in the stratosphere floated reception balloons carrying instruments which reported the least sign of vibration from an enemy aircraft; then having done that they charted to within a few feet the exact position of the plane and thereafter, by contact with the control map, caused moving pointers of light to move exactly over the squares of country being actually traversed by the plane.

And now, as he stood watching the spots of light, Chris saw in a moment how the girl's machines were spreading out in a circle as they left their various starting points, then converged inwards upon London. Immediately, with the help of other officials, he made the necessary disposition of his own forces.

In the meantime, busy before her own instruments, was the girl watching her multi-screens with a feverish earnestness. The infra-red system she used made the moonlit dark as bright as day and gave her a view from any of the fifty machines. London simply lay at her mercy, not in the least concealed by its old-fashioned blackout ... She was alone now too, having dismissed both Irene Grayson and Beatrice, alone as supreme commander of the struggle to enforce her will ...

From the different airfields about London the defenders went up silently into the moonlight, their engines making no sound as swelled to the maximum of power. Keen eyes stared through night sights, searching for what was probably the invisible. From below, even as the planes rose over the city, there came the first monstrous concussion of a falling bomb.

But this was no bomb, surely ... ? It was an earthquake! Entire blocks of buildings crumbled in the onslaught or else rose up piecemeal to disintegrate in mid-air. A crater nearly two miles wide split open to belch forth flames from the disrupted inner seams of the earth. Vastly deep the bomb had penetrated, producing total destruction over an incredibly wide area. In one blow the very heart of the city had crashed in ruin and flame.

Higher went the airmen, and higher, intent on vengeance, searching the empty moonlit wastes for that which they could not see but which radio control from headquarters told them was not very far away. Soon — very soon —

Then out of the emptiness there suddenly flashed a yellow beam. It struck with unerring accuracy, a deadly saffron finger. The pilot who encountered it found himself staring in horrified fascination at his engine as it simply melted out of existence. He felt the beam settle on him. Blinding heat enveloped him. He felt as an insect might feel under the concentrated beam of sunlight from a magnifying glass. Death struck him down before he even glimpsed the flame-dotted basin of doom towards his which shattered machine was streaking.

Time and again, back at control headquarters, Chris Wilson received truncated messages about a yellow beam which struck like lightning from a limitless ceiling and never missed its mark. In ten minutes eleven pilots and planes had crashed to destruction — and the figures mounted alarmingly as the time passed. Chris stood tight-lipped, staring at the operational map whereon was shown only too clearly how the Amazon's fifty machines had completely ringed the city. Time and again too he felt the monstrous gulp and shudder of the earth under the shock of the atomic bombs.

"I'm going up," he announced abruptly. "I can't get to grips with this thing from down here. Take over, Jimmy."

"Right, sir."

The moment he was outside the vastness of the damage being done struck home to Chris. The sky was vermilion from the flame of burning buildings near the airfield. Smuts and sparks came drifting past him: the smell of burning wood and rubber filled the heavy air. Even more deadly was the fact that the falling bombs made no warning swish or whistle with the result that a two-mile crater would suddenly appear to the accompaniment of an overpowering blast before which the most solid of buildings rolled back in a crumbling avalanche of steel and brick.

Chris surveyed it all for a moment, compared it mentally with the films he had seen of the blitz of twenty years before. That had looked like fireworks by comparison. Where the bombs of a European maniac had once demolished buildings, these atomic force creations of a soulless woman lifted out whole streets at once and tore volcanic seams in the crust of the earth. These, in some places spouting cinders and molten matter, only served to render the massacre all the more horrible.

Then, shutting out the horror from his thoughts, Chris raced through the midst of the harassed ground staff to the first machine he could find, and jumped into it. In a few moments he was cleaving the smoky sky at demoniac speed — up and up, eyes glaring through the night sights, his hand taut on the control button which handled both engine and guns. Above him, infinitely high in the sky, yellow beams were sweeping. His eyes narrowed. He tore through the moonlit waste with a speed that nearly stopped his heart … At the point where those beams narrowed to vanishing point there must be a cluster of the attackers.

Faster he went — and faster, his hands gripping the twin switches. He drew to within a mile of the cluster of beams, then fired with everything he had got.

To his amazement nothing happened. Normally, the hail of bullets should have at least put the damned things out of commission; they were armour-piercing. But instead the yellow beams swung round and began to converge on him. There must have been devilishly accurate nightsights on those machines …

Chris dived, twisted and turned downward at top speed before he could be located. Following a trail shaped like an S he twisted towards the fiery spots of colour defiling London … Faster — faster — Back of his mind was the numbing realisation of failure. Nothing that travelled the skies, that he knew of anyway, could deal with these invincibles which saw as clearly in the darkness as in the daylight, which spouted rays of incinerating heat and rained bombs of volcanic violence …

He levelled out, searching for the guides which marked the landing field. Five minutes later he was in communication by radio with the Prime Minister and the emergency committee. Sir Robert Haslam's voice answered him.

"Well, Wilson," he asked anxiously, "how is it going?"

"It's hopeless, sir," he groaned. "Utterly hopeless. For one thing these atomic bombs can't be coped with. They've wrecked half the city already and killed God knows how many people. And those planes up there are invulnerable. I have just been up myself and only just escaped being killed … We're cornered, sir. If this goes on there will not be a plane left by morning, nor one stone on another. We've got to capitulate or die in the worst massacre ever perpetrated by a human hand."

There was a long silence, then the Prime Minister gave a deep sigh.

"Yes, Wilson, you're right," he muttered. "At least accept our thanks for what you and your men have tried to do. I'll send out a message to this woman right away."

In his own headquarters the Prime Minister lifted the radiophone. In a few moments he had contacted the radio stations' control room. A link up was made to his own instrument and he broadcast the capitulation personally, knowing full well that the girl would be listening. He was right, for her reply came over his own radio five minutes later.

"Your capitulation is accepted, Sir Robert — and I will discuss the terms in the morning. I will call off my planes and give you the rest of tonight to put out your fires and clear away the dead and injured. Tomorrow, at ten in the morning, you will convene a meeting of your emergency committee in the House to hear my terms … That is all."

CHAPTER XV

The girl's terms were harsh in the extreme, demanding nothing less than the complete transfer of Governmental control to herself. The question of nomination for election was not even entered into: she took over control by very reason of the power she possessed, that of a conqueror. For the rest she was purely vicious. She sent the Prime Minister to Canada under special escort, assigned Chris Wilson to labouring work in a prison camp, and forced Beatrice into the position of her private secretary ... Such was the sum total of her personal spite, then she turned to more vital matters, using Irene Grayson as her chief consultative scientist.

While the ruins of London were being rebuilt she kept her headquarters in the underground. She drafted bills making all women free to come under her banner, and within limits, to do pretty well as they chose. Most of them formed into special committees to decide on social welfare, supplies, organization, and the hundred and one problems of the community's daily life.

Atomic force too was discussed and planned so that its full benefits could be transferred to the populace for light and heat. At first there was plotting and planning among the angry men for the overthrow of this monstrous woman, until her television eyes, fitted in every prison and every camp, saw and heard all they were doing — then she struck them into silence.

In two months the country was quiet. Abroad, other countries relaxed a little: perhaps this woman would handle things quite well after all. Besides, as long as she remained in England there was nothing to worry about. In any case, ambassadors had reported to their respective Governments; that she was not building armaments, so evidently she had no designs on the rest of the world. Instead she seemed to be deep in plans for industrial redisposition and the turning of atomic force to peaceful uses. After all, she *had* conquered, and was thereby entitled to rule. It might be the sanest course to trade with her and forget other issues.

To the suggestion that trade delegations should come from across the seas the girl was immediately responsive, even cordial. Those who met her in her London headquarters in Whitehall — a truly amazing building equipped with every scientific device — went away impressed by her courtesy, her tolerance, and her extraordinary beauty. But there were some however, keener than the rest, who felt that a woman of such power would not remain satisfied with the mere conquest of Britain …

One morning when Vi and Irene Grayson were at work in the office there was a knock at the door and Beatrice came in.

"Anything the matter?" Vi asked sharply. "We're extremely busy."

Bee came forward slowly to the desk.

"I've just been thinking — since I'm in this regime now for better or worse — that I might be able to help with some suggestions. For instance, there is a communication this morning from a group of industrialists, most of them having taken over industries originally run by men. Cynthia Drew is at the head of the group and she poses a rather serious question …"

"Well?"

"The group wants to know what you are going to do about the future. What, for one thing, is to happen to the race to come? As things stand now, with homes broken up and men and women separated, there will be no children for the future. What are you going to do?"

"That's puzzled me, too," Irene Grayson admitted, thinking. "In your proclamation when you took over you said that for the purpose of marriage and child you would permit men and women, specially selected and married by a eugenics committee, to spend six months together at chosen times. You've said no more since, though."

"That was just temporary mollification," Vi shrugged. "I have no real intention of allowing men and women to mingle for three years at least. Statistics show that it will not be necessary until then to think of the future. There are far too many children as it is. Weeding out will do good."

"These industrialists will demand a better answer than that," Bee said seriously.

"What else am I to do?"

"I think," Bee said, thinking, "that I have a solution."

"*You* have!" Vi gazed at her in surprise. "Just what?"

"Synthesis."

Vi exchanged an astonished glance with Irene Grayson.

"Why not?" Bee insisted. "I've read enough of the activities of scientists to know that they have been trying for years to create life in a test tube. Surely you, with your superhuman knowledge of scientific laws, could do it? In that way, as I see it, you could give an infinite number of people to the world — men or women, which you decide — and thereby there would never be any need again for men or women to mingle for the purely biological purpose of producing their own kind. In any case, it is a very primitive function … isn't it?"

Vi was silent, staring absently in front of her.

"Synthesis," she repeated at last, slowly. "Truly it has been said that out of the mouths of babes and sucklings. That you should get such an idea! Now I know it was worth my while to spare your life and keep you beside me. The obvious solution!" Her eyes gleamed suddenly. "What scientists have failed to do so far I can certainly accomplish! The idea is a masterpiece!"

"But isn't it an intensely difficult job?" Irene Grayson questioned. "I dabbled in it myself before turning to atomic force and couldn't get a thing out of it."

"It's difficult, but not insurmountable," Vi said, her eyes gleaming with excitement. "With my mastery of science I believe I could conquer the problem. Yes — I could give an infinite number of women to the world — wonderful women, freed of all hereditary tendency, women without parents, trained and patterned by scientific power! A race of super-women … What could I *not* do with a secret like that! All the old animalistic process of male and female union swept aside — all the old rubbishy formula of love of man for woman destroyed. There is no love in science — only progress and established fact!"

There was a silence. Irene Grayson and Beatrice exchanged glances. It was clear the girl had become completely obsessed by the idea.

"Are you sure that a synthetic woman — or man — would be such a benefit as you suppose?" Irene, Grayson mused. "Suppose he or she turned into a monster and destroyed you?"

"You, a scientist, say that!" the girl cried in scorn. "I know that idea was once rampant, sponsored no doubt by Shelley's Frankenstein, but in these days we know that a synthetically created human being would be ultra-perfect, not ultra-dangerous. It would have no human ills to overcome; no hereditary tendencies to inherit. It would be perfect, faultless, teachable. The synthetic woman of my designing will be a genius, beautiful —" Vi straightened up suddenly. "I shall begin experiments immediately," she announced. "In the meantime, Bee, inform these industrialists that their question is being considered and that an early reply will be given. You know how to handle it."

Beatrice nodded a quiet assent; then Vi turned to Irene Grayson.

"Irene, you take over for a while. I've got to shut myself away in the laboratory to work out the details."

With that she hurried away, all else forgotten for the moment. Beatrice and Irene looked at each other again — serious, half-puzzled looks on both their faces. Then with an odd little smile Beatrice turned also and went out to her own office …

*

It was a fortnight before Vi emerged from her experiment in synthesis with a smile of triumph on her face. When she summoned Irene Grayson and Beatrice into her office they found her pacing up and down in an ecstasy that bordered on excitement.

"I have it!" she announced. "I have definitely got the secret! Synthetic flesh itself is easy enough to make — combination of calcium, phosphorus, and other ingredients of the human body — but to knit those elements up into the exact formation of a human being, nerve for nerve, vein for vein, has demanded a good deal of care. That too I have mastered, and at any moment I choose I can produce life!"

"How?" Irene Grayson asked, awed in spite of herself. "What is it that has so long baulked scientists from making the supreme discovery?"

"They did not use cosmic rays — but I did! Cosmic rays are known to be mainly responsible for evolution. Down here on the surface of the earth they are lessened in intensity by the layers of atmosphere, of course, but in these days of stratoflight it is simple to send an experimental globe to the limit of the atmosphere. I did just that! I sent up a globe containing a quantity of synthetic flesh, sent it up so high that it became soaked in pure, unscreened cosmic rays. It came down *alive*! Alive, I say, with its cells somehow excited into the chemical reaction which we call life! That one living piece of synthetic flesh is the clue to all the rest. Don't you see? Once I have completed this synthetic woman in every detail I have but to send up the cold clay into the stratosphere in a globe and so bring her to life! After that …" Vi clenched her fists. "After that there is nothing to stop me making women by the thousand — mass produce them! Special giant laboratories for the purpose …"

"In that case," Irene Grayson said, thinking, "you can dispense with ordinary human beings?"

"There is nothing I cannot do!" Vi retorted. "Think of it! Endless legions of women who do not know the meaning of sex, women who are such in outline alone but otherwise totally neuter. Man, as a sex, totally exterminated. Women who will form the armies of the future … I can conquer the Earth! I can reach out to other worlds — to the ends of the universe, make the name of the Golden Amazon a symbol of dread and power!"

Irene and Beatrice studied the burning ambition in the girl's violet eyes for a moment. Then she gave an impatient gesture.

"Well, why don't you say something?" she demanded. "Does the scope of my plans alarm you, or what?"

"I was wondering," Irene said slowly, "how our followers are going to react to the news. We understand the scientific progress you are introducing, but they don't."

"Why wonder over that? I am offering to women the conquest of the universe, nothing less. To conquer it in our name!"

"But you are not," Irene contradicted. "Women, as a sex, will die out along with men. Finally nothing but artificial creatures will stalk the country, and finally the world, with you at the supreme head. Cold, merciless, scientific beings who at your behest will destroy and dominate wherever they go — pitiless, because they will not have a single human characteristic. Ruthless, because like a machine they will not be able to distinguish between good and bad. I begin to wonder if you are not trying to reach too far. Mastery of one country is one thing, the extermination of men and women and replacement by synthetic ones is very different …"

"I believe in it," Bee said simply. "I see now how wrong I've been in the past, how I've misjudged Vi. If we are out to conquer everything — and we are — what on earth does the method matter?"

Vi flashed her a grateful look and Irene Grayson looked at her sharply puzzling. Then she gave a shrug.

"Well, maybe because I'm older than either of you I'm a bit more conservative. Perhaps it's right when it comes to it — How long will it take you to finish this experimental woman?"

"She will be ready in three weeks. I've calculated it exactly. In the meantime, Bee, you had better answer that question from the industrialists. Tell them that synthetic beings will take the place of children and that the race will be maintained that way. At the same time, I have some new decrees which I shall want you to draft. — All the medically unfit will be destroyed, man or woman. All female children will be removed to State creches at times and in the manner I shall later appoint … You see, as time goes on it will become necessary to employ tens of thousands of young women as scientists to teach these female babies the doctrine I intend to institute. All men up to sixty will do labouring work, irrespective of their former attainments. Those that have been exempt up to now for health reasons will be put to work immediately since a great deal of building and expansion is ahead of us. Male children too must be turned over to the State and completely segregated from female children. Their education will be confined exclusively to the development of their physical power: their mentalities will be bent into accepting complete subservience to the female who in adult life will rule them …"

The girl meditated, her lips tight. Then she nodded slowly.

"Yes, I think that covers everything. As a consequence, all the old sordid existence of love and lust will cease. Man and woman will finally be separated for ever. Ahead of us are vast conquests, so vast that they cannot be handled while men and women are attracted towards each other."

"Aren't you afraid that you may produce discontent among your followers by launching such sweeping decrees?" Bee asked.

"They will only be issued one at a time, consolidate as we go, so to speak. And while the rest of the world is trying to puzzle out what I am driving at I will build up enough power to withstand and destroy any onslaught that may be directed towards me. I am fully aware that to impose my will will mean violent struggles — but I shall win them … Anyway, Bee, you know what to do. Draft those decrees, and at the close of the three weeks when I have completed this synthetic woman I will issue them in complete — and where necessary amended — form. In the meantime," Vi added, "instruct my airwomen to prepare for manoeuvres at ten o'clock in the morning of that day — that is October fifteenth. If there is any dissent concerning my decrees the squadrons will act as a reminder that I am dictatress. Now, Irene, what do you think of my plans?"

"Excellent — and ambitious," she said quietly, but she seemed to be thinking of something else.

Vi nodded and turned to the door. "You two carry on, then. I have much to do."

*

Chris Wilson peered at the note he had received surreptitiously as he had entered his cell in the prison camp. It had been smuggled into his hand by a fellow prisoner but in the dim light he had not had the chance to see his face. Not that that mattered: it was the note which counted. Thoughtfully he studied it.

"*You have only to destroy the Golden Amazon's hundred planes in order to snatch her most dangerous weapon from her hands. With so many other projects on hand she cannot replace them quickly. The hundred planes will manoeuvre on October 15th at 10 a.m. over London. The one machine to destroy these others is the* Ultra. *If this machine is obtained for you and placed at the Surrey ford road — ten miles from your prison at 4 a.m. on the morning of October 15th, you should be able to fly it. Destroy those planes and the Amazon is powerless to enforce her will for some time to come. Underground workers have got this note to you. Do not fail. Get out of your camp somehow!*"

"Get out!" Chris breathed. "I'll say I will, even if it kills me! Ten o'clock over London on October 15th … Bee wrote this. It must be her, despite her effort to disguise her writing. Yes, I'll get out …

CHAPTER XVI

At nine thirty in the morning of October 15ᵗʰ, Vi came into her main office with the announcement that her experiment was finished, that the first synthetic woman only needed sending into the stratosphere in order to come to life. Tomorrow perhaps … Then she turned to matters on hand.

"You drafted those decrees, Beatrice?" she asked.

"Yes — and I arranged for the manoeuvres you wanted this morning."

"Good!" Vi looked at the planes circling the sky outside, then she turned as Cynthia Drew was announced.

Vi looked rather irritated but extended her hand cordially enough as the woman industrialist came in.

"This is an unexpected pleasure, Miss Drew —"

"I think," Cynthia Drew said, "we can dispense with the pleasantries. My visit is a serious one."

"Oh?" Vi's expression changed. "Why? What is the trouble?"

"Those decrees of yours! They're monstrous! Synthetic women indeed! All children to be handed over to the State; men and women to be segregated just to please your whim! That isn't rulership — it's insanity!"

Vi's cold eyes strayed from Cynthia Drew's angry face to Beatrice. But she was looking out of the window as though not heeding the conversation.

"When did *you* receive notice of my decrees?" Vi asked ominously.

"At the same time as your answer to our question concerning the future of the race — three weeks ago. I know they were only draft decrees subject to amendment, but in essence they were serious enough to show your ultimate objective. I called a conference of leading women immediately. We unanimously decided to oppose the decrees. You don't seem to realise what you are doing! You have incurred the fury of every married woman in the land, the anger of those about to be married when you took control and forbade any such action. I considered it my duty to publish those draft decrees of yours in my own newspaper under the heading — 'Where is the Amazon Leading Us?' Support for your ideas averaged ten per cent of the population. The rest are in opposition."

Vi stood in grim silence for a moment; then abruptly she swung round and seized Bee's arm with such savagery she cried out:

"You!" Vi glared into her face. "You did it! You had no authority to send out drafts until I had had the chance to check them and make amendments —"

"They represented your real intentions!" Bee retorted, her eyes flashing. "Where was the purpose of starting out mildly and then building up to the real issue later on? I know you planned to do it that way and build up your own means of enforcing your will in the meantime. I decided otherwise and sent the decrees out. And why? Because I knew they would outrage every decent woman in the land! And I was right!"

"This synthesis idea was yours in the first place," Vi said slowly.

"Yes, I know." Bee smiled bitterly. "I suggested it to you because I knew that while it would appeal to your cold, scientific senses it would horrify most normal women, myself included. I knew you would be here this morning to see the manoeuvres and report the success of your experiment, so I suggested to Miss Drew that she should call in and see you … I hate you, Vi — hate you as I've never hated anybody in my life before! I did it for revenge, to expose you for the fiend you really are! My mother and father died because of you and if I die too as the result of this it doesn't matter. Maybe I'll have done something to straighten out the ghastly mess you have made of society and the lives of formerly happy men and women …"

An arrogant smiled crossed Vi's face.

"You always were a snivelling little fool, Bee — and this day's work will cost you dear before I'm finished with you. As for you, Miss Drew, my decrees remain!"

"Not with my sanction!" she retorted. "We know you have supreme power but your decrees have convinced everybody that you aim at scientific despotism. You are bringing about, if you can, the strangulation of the human race and the exploitation of present day children for your own devilish purposes. That we will not allow."

"Remember, Miss Drew, there are other women who can fill your place if you get in my way —"

"Not now there aren't. You've poisoned all your former followers. It has become evident to everybody just where you intend your rule to finish."

"You listen to me," Vi said slowly. "The control of this country is in my hands, and those who see fit to work against me can be destroyed. I shall have synthetic women to take their places anyway, and synthetic men if I am driven to it. I shall remove you from industrial control, Miss Drew, and I shall hound you out of the country. Whichever of your contemporaries sees fit to show opposition will share the same fate. In case you have forgotten my power, look out of this window!"

She pointed to the flyers just commencing their manoeuvres as the big electric clock in the square below indicated ten o'clock.

Cynthia Drew gave a cynical smile. "Further bombing will not alter the opinion of the vast majority of women now against you, Miss Brant, rest assured of that ... I suppose those machines are flying around as a threat?"

"They are flying to remind whatever fools there are like you that I have the whip hand!" Vi retorted. "I admit I had only intended to announce synthesis this morning, and my other decrees one by one later on. I had expected trouble even with the synthesis announcement, hence the planes. I —"

She broke off sharply and stared above. Then she gave a sudden start and looked fixedly through the glass.

"What — what is that?" she cried hoarsely.

For into the midst of the circling flyers there had swept a machine far larger than any of them, glittering in the morning sunshine. It blazed forth as it moved with twin electrical beams, caught two of the flyers amidships and sent their plates twirling in pieces through the sky. Damaged beyond repair, the woman pilots killed instantly, the machines screamed down in a spiral dive towards the city, vanished with remote concussions as they fell to the east amidst a huddle of buildings.

"My *Ultra*!" Vi screamed abruptly. "My ship — !"

She jumped back as though struck as that grey thunderbolt swerved round with diabolical speed and came tearing back. It decimated two more ships on the way — then the others, aware of the danger, gathered into formation and swept upwards with their yellow rays bristling.

"Fools!" Vi shrieked. "Fools! You can't penetrate the *Ultra* — !"

She whirled round and slammed in the radio switch on her desk. But there was no answer in the loud speaker. For some reason all contact was dead … Stunned, she turned to look at Irene Grayson and Beatrice — but they were watching the sky intently with Cynthia Drew.

Vi joined them again and stood watching in helpless fury as flyer after flyer, outmatched by the superior weapons and faster speed of the *Ultra*, went smashing to destruction. Wherever they went, however high they climbed, death was after them, and all the concentrated onslaught of their yellow beams had no effect on the armour-plated hull.

Down they hurtled, in twos and threes, in whole groups of flying metal as the electric guns swept the length of their formations. Then at last the survivors, a woeful twenty or so, turned and fled; streaking away from London towards the coast. The *Ultra* followed them a little distance, brought down three more, then it returned and began a steady patrol at five miles height.

Vi stood quite still for a long time, absorbing the shock. Then all of a sudden she swung round in blind fury and seized Beatrice in a grip of iron, bore her backwards and pinned her against the wall.

"You did this!" she screamed at her. "You did it! Admit it! You released Chris Wilson! Only he could fly a machine in that fashion! That stinking, low down pilot lover of yours, who has always been mixed up in some intrigue against me! You knew where he was. You knew where the *Ultra* was! As my secretary you knew everything — Damn you, Bee, speak the truth or I'll crush every bone in your miserable little body — !"

Bee got a stinging slap in the face that sent her reeling sideways. Immediately Vi had hold of her again, her eyes blazing with unholy fury.

"Answer me!" she screamed.

"I didn't!" Bee panted hoarsely, her eyes wide. "In all truth I didn't! I sent the decrees, yes; I've admitted it. But I didn't do this — Honestly!"

"Why, you cheap little liar —" Suddenly Vi had her by the throat, forced her tight against the wall and tightened her fingers with all their superhuman power. Bee struggled desperately as she felt herself choking …

Then Vi felt something prod her in the small of the back.

"Let her go!"

Vi hesitated, then gradually relaxed her grip as she saw her own flame gun pointing at her. She remembered it had been in the desk drawer. She followed the hand holding the gun, up to the quiet eyes of Irene Grayson.

"Even *you* turn against me?" Vi's voice was nearly inaudible.

Irene Grayson did not speak. She waited until the gasping Beatrice had moved over to a chair and fallen into it, fingering her bruised throat. Vi watched her narrowly, then stood erect and eyed the gun. Suddenly she dived for it, but it went off instantly and fired searing flame across her right shoulder. Her uniform was charred from collar to elbow and the flesh beneath burned and blackened from the flame. With a little gasp of pain she fell against the heavy desk, her right arm hanging limply at her side.

"Bee spoke the truth," Irene Grayson stated, staring over the desk. "She did not arrange the destruction of your air force: I did that! I did it when I knew what you intended doing with those decrees. She told me of what she proposed to do to expose you, and I agreed with her. We decided to strike simultaneously to break you. I got a message through to Chris Wilson by the underground factions against you. I had it all arranged for Wilson to get the *Ultra* since of course I knew as well as Bee where it was concealed. I also cut off the radio so you could not send orders to your pilots …"

Vi was silent, mastering a storm of emotion — then suddenly Bee gave a shriek.

"*Look at her!*"

But the others were doing that already — fascinatedly. Vi was changing incredibly. Her hands were no longer golden and supple but like yellow claws, becoming thinner with every moment. The most incredible metamorphosis was taking place in her face. The cold, aloof beauty of it was smearing, like a sponge drawn over a priceless painting. Her round chin was becoming pointed; her cheeks deep and sunken as though from starvation. Bemused, she still stood there, clasping her injured shoulder, quivering under the strain of a vast nervous shock.

"What's — what's wrong in here?" she whispered, staring vacantly in front of her. "Where am I? It's so dark — so quiet. Speak — somebody!" she implored hoarsely. "Don't leave me alone!"

"She's — dying!" Cynthia Drew whispered, horrified.

Vi turned her head a little, then she fell to the floor and tried futilely to rise, clutching at her throat. Words died on her lips. She turned over and dropped flat on her face.

For a moment or two there was a deadly silence, then Irene Grayson moved over and raised the girl's head and shoulders in her arms. She could not help a shudder at the shock she received. Behind her, Bee gave a little gasp of horror and turned away.

It was no longer the superb Golden Amazon who lay breathing shallowly on the floor — but an old, incredibly ugly hag, her face a tracery of seams, her blind eyes just burned-out coals. The once waving golden hair was snow white, the supple body thin beyond belief. Age, incredible age, was stamped there.

For a moment or two she lay motionless in Irene Grayson's arms, then with a little shudder life was gone. Slowly, very slowly, Irene Grayson released her hold and stood up again.

*

There was a long silence until at last Irene Grayson spoke again — tonelessly. "From the moment I knew of this girl's scheme for the ultimate domination of the universe, from the moment I knew she was a scientific genius with no soul or womanly instinct, I decided to break her power. I did it with the help of Bee who was pledged to the same cause. She incited the people against her and I destroyed the means of her enforcing her will. A provisional Government can now take control until the ex-Prime Minister can be flown back from Canada. The regime of Violet Ray Brant is ended …

"It has not been easy for me," Irene went on, her voice low. "Far from it! I only did it really because she meant more to me than anything else in the world — and for that reason I had to stop her mad onrush to doom."

There was a puzzled, expectant silence.

"This girl — this lifeless creature — was my daughter!"

The statement made Beatrice jerk up her head in astonishment, while Cynthia Drew's eyes became incredulous behind her glasses.

"Yes, my daughter," Irene Grayson repeated gravely. "I knew it for perhaps the first time when Bee mentioned to me in a private chat that Vi had been found near Little Beading. I became sure of it when it was stated at the Nomination Meeting that a Dr. Axton of Little Beading had operated — or at least had been presumed to have operated — on a baby girl in that district. You see, in those days of the blitz Little Beading was only a village. It had one school, to which my little girl had been sent as an evacuee. On the night of the air raid the school was destroyed at the same time Axton lost his life. My inquiry over twenty years ago showed that every child had been accounted for except mine. She was listed among the missing.

"But there had been found a doctor's coat, and in it a pocket book giving the name of Prout. In Parliament it was stated that Prout was a close friend of Axton. Suddenly, for me, everything tied up. I realised many things — her scientific loves, inherited from me; the awful experiment which had changed her from a lovable, happy child into an almost sexless demon of a woman with superhuman strength. It had to be her: the coincidence was too obvious for any other conclusion. That was why I ceased to support her in Parliament from that moment. Only her name of Violet Ray puzzled me. The 'Brant' was explained easily enough, but the rest was a mystery. 'Ray' might fit into Grayson, of course. Anyhow, her real name was Marjorie Grayson."

Irene Grayson reflected a moment, then compressing her lips she turned and pressed a button on the desk. Three armed women came in.

"Remove her," Irene said quietly — then when the door had closed she relaxed and gave a moody smile.

"My sympathies are with you, Mrs. Grayson," Cynthia Drew said, her eyes serious. "I realise how you must feel."

"One thing I would ask of you," Irene said quietly. "Do not reveal to the world that I am the mother of — of that! That I brought her to defeat, and her death — with the help of you, Bee — can be mentioned, of course, but there let it stop. She was my daughter, until science changed her." Beatrice and Cynthia Drew nodded silent acquiescence, then the door opened again and Chris Wilson appeared. Eagerly he looked from one to the other.

"Well, did it work? Did we succeed?"

"We won," Bee smiled, moving forward to embrace him. "And we have to thank this lady here, Mrs. Grayson, for it." Chris looked at Irene in surprise.

"I don't quite understand. I thought that Bee —"

"It was I who sent you that note, Mr. Wilson. I am — or rather was — Miss Brant's chief assistant. You more than fulfilled my hopes in destroying those planes … Now you have fresh instructions. I am temporarily in authority and Miss Brant — the Golden Amazon — is dead …"

"Dead!" Chris exclaimed. "But how on earth …"

Irene briefly outlined the circumstances.

"Presumably," she finished, "the emotional shock and physical injury brought the end of her furious life energy. Anyway, I will control a provisional Government until Sir Robert Haslam can be brought back from Canada to take over. I'd suggest you use the *Ultra* and leave immediately for Canada. Fetch him back right away."

Chris nodded promptly. "Okay, I'll do that — and in a machine like that I'll do it in record time … Bye for the moment, Bee — and when I come back you and I have a lot to catch up on!"

With that he hurried off and Irene looked at the two women with a faint smile.

"We have a job ahead of us clearing up Marjorie's — I mean Vi's affairs, haven't we?" she asked slowly. "She was a mighty busy girl with massive ideas …"

Bee came forward and laid a hand on her arm.

"Irene, we're both sorry for the blow Vi's death must have dealt you. We realise that in spite of all she did she was your child. If there is anything we can do …"

"You can help me best by forgetting the whole thing. I have come to the conclusion that my daughter did die in the 1940 blitz. That cruel, ambitious woman was not my little girl but a product of scientific ambition, an experiment which gave her many years of being a wonderwoman. Then outraged Nature took revenge and destroyed her horribly! But she gave us great inventions which will live hereafter — cold light, synthesis, transmutation of base metals, equality for women, aviation … Against such monumental discoveries my own contribution of atomic force will seem footling. I shall remember her for those things — always." She became silent — and outside the city too seemed to have become quiet…

22684631R00095

Printed in Great Britain
by Amazon